Child of Fire

A.S.Chambers

Acknowledgements

For all my Patreon and Kickstarter supporters who helped me financially and emotionally in the creation of the book.

With special mention to the following:
Fiona, Tish Toglet, Elyssa Long, Paul Laters, Rebecca Benson, Holley, Karen Woodham, Ariion Dragoa, Melissa, Paul and Mark, Gemma Innes, Charlie Cummings, Kevin Denwood, Debs McGowan (SteamGoth), Lee, Simon Brindley, Ron Chick, Martje.

Thank you, you wonderful readers!

Also, a huge thanks to Rachel Lowe for beta reading this outing of the Twins as well as Child of Light. Their input really helped, bringing the insight and perspective of a teenager.

Also by A.S.Chambers

Sam Spallucci Series.
The Casebook of Sam Spallucci – 2012
Sam Spallucci: Ghosts From The Past – 2014
Sam Spallucci: Shadows of Lancaster – 2016
Sam Spallucci: The Case of The Belligerent Bard – 2016
Sam Spallucci: Dark Justice – 2018
Sam Spallucci: Troubled Souls – 2020
Sam Spallucci: Bloodline - Prologues & Epilogue – 2021
Sam Spallucci: Bloodline – 2021
Sam Spallucci: Fury of the Fallen – 2022
Sam Spallucci: Lux Æterna – 2024
Sam Spallucci: Dare The Dragon – Due 2026

Short Story Anthologies.
Oh Taste And See – 2014
All Things Dark And Dangerous – 2015
Let All Mortal Flesh – 2016
Mourning Has Broken – 2018
Hide Not Thou Thy Face – 2020
If Ye Loathe Me – 2022
Out Of The Depths – 2024
Hear My Scare – 2025

Ebook short stories.
High Moon – 2013
Girls Just Wanna Have Fun – 2013
Needs Must – 2019

Novellas.
Songbird – 2019
Bobby Normal and The Eternal Talisman – 2021
Bobby Normal and the Virtuous Man – 2021
Bobby Normal and the Children of Cain – 2022
Bobby Normal and The Fallen – 2023
Bobby Normal and the Black Dragon – 2024
Child of Light – 2024

Omnibuses.
Children of Cain – 2019
Macabre Collection: Volume One – 2022
Macabre Collection: Volume Two – 2023
Sam Spallucci Omnibus: Volume One – 2022
Sam Spallucci Omnibus: Volume Two – 2024
The Adventures of Bobby Normal – 2024

Contents

Chapter One   1

Chapter Two   15

Chapter Three   30

Chapter Four   48

Chapter Five   61

Chapter Six   77

Chapter Seven   101

Epilogue   111

Author's Notes   113

About The Author   119

Chapter One

"Come to me, come to me, my child…"

The familiar stone staircase is cold under my bare feet. My white nightgown provides very little protection from the chill night air and goosebumps prickle my skin as I climb ever higher. There is no handrail, so I am forced to reach out with my left hand and steady myself as best as I can against the crumbling stone masonry of the tower. The only light I possess comes from the small candle I hold in my right hand, its tiny flame guttering and dancing in the breeze. My heart is pounding and I feel sick with terror but I know that there is no way back now. All I can do is climb ever higher.

All I can do is climb towards the voice.

"Come to me, come to me, my child…"

I hear it again from higher up the spiral staircase. It is quiet, masculine and reassuring.

Yet it terrifies me.

The candle flickers and I make to scream out, desperate not to be plunged into darkness, but the flame survives, allowing me to glimpse the top of the staircase. There is a door there, an old wooden door. It looks like it has been made from strips of a large tree and has two enormous, black hinges to the left. Steadying myself, I snatch my hand away from the wall and reach out only to find out to my horror that there is no handle.

"Come to me, come to me, my child…"

The voice is more insistent this time. It is calling from behind the door, but I can't reach it. I can't break through. There is a deep rumbling sound behind me and I feel the tower begin to shake. Just as it always does, the staircase is beginning to collapse. I hammer on the door with my free hand but no one answers. I cry out that I want to come in, that I want to walk through this door, to escape the tower that is falling apart around me.

But no one answers and the stairs continue to crumble away behind me.

I scream louder and louder. As I do, the flame on the candle increases in size and the cold that had pursued me up the stairs is no more. The fire is not just burning atop the small wax stick, but deep inside of me.

I press my hand firmly against the wood of the door as the last of the stairs crack apart behind me and I concentrate, feeling the all-consuming heat building up within me…

I wake with a start, my heart thumping in my chest. Gasping in the cold morning air, I begin to untangle my legs from my twisted duvet. As I do so, my eyes dart around me, taking in the reassuring surroundings of my room. There's Floof, the giant furry bear that Mike won for me last summer. He sits quietly on my armchair, unconcerned about my nightmare. There's the blue dress Dad bought me for the *Kidsweek* ball this coming weekend. It's hanging from the hook on the back of my bedroom door.

A door that *definitely* has a handle… There's my phone, plugged into its cradle, happily charging away. Next to it is a glass of water. I swallow and wince. As usual, my throat is sore, as if I'd actually been screaming. I lift myself up and grab the glass on my bedside table. Sipping the water, I grimace. It's warm. Why is it always warm?

Anyway, warm water aside, this is my life. My *normal* life. There are no crazy voices here or creepy staircases. This is the room of a normal teenage girl.

I swallow.

I snatch my mobile out of its cradle, flick it on and navigate to a webpage I bookmarked weeks ago. The voice of a woman speaks: "I've had an email from Amanda in Sale who keeps having this repeating dream of walking up a dark staircase, holding nothing but a candle then, when she reaches the top, there is a door that has no handle, yet she knows she has to get to the other side. All the time, she keeps hearing a man's voice that she does not recognise calling her name. She keeps waking with a start and is out of sorts for the rest of the day."

Well, that's an understatement. When the dreams started, about three months ago, they were every couple of weeks and I felt awful for the rest of the day. I felt like I was going to walk into school and have a surprise Physics test sprung on me. I *hate* Physics. I would spend the whole day just waiting for something bad to happen. Then the dreams started to move closer together until they were once a week. That was when I found the podcast, *Let's Talk*. It was full of weirdos writing into the lady who hosted it with all their stupid stories. At first, I just listened, telling myself to be glad that I wasn't one of those losers. But then, one morning, I woke up in a blind panic and I realised that I had no one to talk to. Sure, Mum and Dad are great, but they'd just fuss, like they do. So I emailed the lady.

"Amanda, don't worry. You're not alone. This sort of thing happens all the time. Yes, it can feel upsetting and disturbing, but it's just the brain firing off random images. I have a similar one myself." Now, every time I have one of the dreams, I listen to her voice and it helps to calm me. I actually emailed her again last week to say how it was great that she helped but then I realised that there hadn't been a new podcast since January. I guess she gave up.

People do that, don't they? If things are hard, you just give up. Why should you bother putting effort into something when it takes so much time? There could be other things you could be doing. My eyes wander back over to the blue dress hanging on the back of my bedroom door. Yeah, life is definitely for living, not stressing.

Talking of which.

I swing my legs out of bed, stretch and start to get ready for the day. I wander through to my bathroom and, once I've showered, massaging out the aches of the night, I sit in front of my dressing table, blow-drying my hair. As I stretch out the blonde I grimace at the sight of the roots starting to show. Don't get the wrong idea here. I'm not some peroxide tart. I *am* actually blonde. It's my natural colour. It's just…

Well, there's another colour mixed in with it. I don't like it. It got me called names when I was younger, so I dye it out now, but I swear to God it keeps growing back quicker. It's okay, though. I have an appointment booked with Mum's hairdresser tomorrow, Saturday, so it'll look awesome again for the *Kidsweek* ball. I reckon I'll just have to ignore those small streaks for the day, so I get dressed before heading downstairs for breakfast.

I love breakfast. It's a great time of the day. The sun shines in through the kitchen window and there's the satisfying aroma of eggs and bacon as Mum cooks us up something hearty. I slide up onto the tall stool by the breakfast bar and down my OJ in one. A refreshing *cold* drink, thank God!

"Hey, Sweetie!" Mum calls over her shoulder as she does every morning whilst flipping the bacon. "You sleep okay?"

"Mmhmm," I say as I swallow the juice. "Absolutely." I always push the image of a door with no handle out of my head. I don't want her worrying.

"That's great," she smiles as she slips the bacon and the eggs onto my plate, next to some buttered toast. "There you go. Eat up." And, she stands there, smiling, as I devour the lot.

Well, almost the lot.

"Morning, Princess!" I get the familiar scent of Dad's strong aftershave as he kisses the top of my head whilst pinching a slice of bacon off my plate.

"Dad!" I protest with mock seriousness and he winks at me whilst chewing on the fried pig. Picking up his stuff from the end of the breakfast bar, he gives Mum a peck on the cheek and heads off to work.

I'm grinning to myself as I finish off the cooked part of my breakfast and grab the box of cornflakes that sits waiting, as always, on the counter. As the crisp little flakes tumble into my bowl, I think about how perfect my family is, how it's just like those families you see in cornflake commercials. In fact, I'd go so far as to say that we're like the cornflakes themselves: little islands of tranquillity in a perfect bowl of calm.

Okay, so perhaps my simile isn't perfect, but you get the idea. My family is great and I love my life.

I finish off my breakfast, grab my stuff for school and head off for another perfect day.

Well, at least, I hope it will be.

It's all starting out as normal. Mike meets me at the end of the road as usual. "Hey, you," he grins as I wrap my arm around him. "You good?"

"Sure. Even better now. You?"

He bends down and kisses me. "Oh, absolutely," he continues to grin as he pulls back and we head off to school. We've been going out for a year now. He asked me out last *Kidsweek*. So, the ball this weekend will be our anniversary. Some kids call us an old married couple and make like they're throwing up when they see us kissing, but they're just jealous because Mike's such a catch. He came to the school last March and we immediately hit it off. He's in the same art and PE classes as me and he's really good at both. Not only can he play rugby, but he can draw really well. He did a sketch of me about a week after he started at our school and gave it to me. No one has ever drawn me before so, when he asked if he could be my date to last year's *Kidsweek* ball, of course I said yes. Who wouldn't?

"You looking forward to tomorrow?"

I rub my head against Mike's shoulder. "Oh, I don't know. I was thinking of staying at home and washing my hair…"

"Oh."

I look up at his crystal blue eyes and laugh at the worry in them. "You idiot. Of course I'm not washing my hair. Well, not all night, anyway. I'm going to the ball with you."

His face lights up. "Oh! That's great! I thought… I dunno… Perhaps you weren't?"

"You great lunk. I've been looking forward to this all month." So we carry on walking to school, chatting about stuff, complaining about teachers and rubbishing people we don't like.

It's as we walk down Marsland Road and near school that Mike feels my arm tighten around his waist.

"You okay?" he asked.

We carry on walking up to the gates but my eyes are fixed on the opposite side of the road. "Can't they do anything about *him*?"

Mike's eyes follow mine. There, sitting slumped against the wall, next to the sign for Beaufort Road, is the *Creep*. He first turned up just over a month ago, at the end of February. One morning he was just sitting there, staring straight ahead. Well, I say *staring*… It's kind of hard to tell as you can't see his face; it's all wrapped in bandages and he has these really dark sunglasses fixed permanently in the wrappings. He wears a long dirty coat. It was probably originally a cream colour, but it's stained and grubby, as if he's been sleeping in it in a park or somewhere, you know, like tramps and vages do. He has a woolly hat pulled down tight over his bandaged head and he wears a pair of thick gloves on his hands. Becky Ashcroft (she's in my English Lit set) says that he's a war vet who snapped and killed all his squad out in Afghanistan. She says he set a bomb off to do it and got badly burnt, hence all the bandages. Mind you, she also says that the world is flat and that the king is really a lizard, so I'm not sure she's a reliable source.

But, the Creep is definitely that, *a creep*, so perhaps she's right on this one. I don't know for sure. What I do know is that he scares me. I feel the same cold chill that I have when I'm walking up the crumbling staircase in my nightmares. "Can't they do anything about him?" I repeat.

Mike shrugs. "The teachers used to go out and talk to him when he first turned up, didn't they? The police came that time to move him on. But he just came back. He's not done anything, so they've just left him to it."

"Left him to *what*, though?" I snap. "I bet he's perving on us."

I feel Mike's arm pulling me and he guides me into the safety of the schoolyard. As he does, I'm convinced that the Creep's masked eyes are burning into my back.

"Amanda!"

The sound of my name being called out pulls me away from the feeling that the Creep is perving on me. I grin as Laura Walker practically bounces up the school drive towards us. Laura and I go way back. She's probably my oldest friend. We've known each other since primary school and have been more or less inseparable since we were five. She's a great friend and her family have this nice house on the edge of town. It's not too big, just a five-bedroom job with three reception rooms and a reasonably sized garden and pool. I like hanging out there over the summer hols — that is when they're not over in the South of France in their little holiday home. It's so sweet. They've taken me out there a few times. It has a maid and everything. There are some lovely little shops down the road. When we were little, Laura's parents used to let us wander down on our own and order *baguettes* from the *boulangerie*. They're so liberal. I love them.

"So?" Laura is practically bouncing up and down, her cute red braids jumping animatedly on the shoulders of her blazer, as we walk up the drive to the schoolyard. "Have you heard?"

"What?"

"Georgia's going to the ball with Edgar."

"No way!"

"Yes way."

I roll my eyes. "She's such a slut. What about Jay?"

"Guess she dumped him."

"Like I said. Slut."

Laura nodded, her braids bouncing again on her school blazer. "I wonder who it'll be next week?"

I shrug. "Some other poor sucker. She's had them swarming around her like flies around you-know-what since she put that post on her socials."

"The one of her on the beach?"

I nod.

"Slut," Laura says.

"Slut," I agree.

"What post?" Mike asks.

I pat his arm. "It's okay, Baby. Nothing for you to worry about."

"Okay," he grins and wraps his arm tighter around me.

I smile up at the handsome face of the love of my life before crying out as someone bangs into my shoulder. "Hey!"

The student vaguely turns round, barely acknowledges me with a *couldn't care less* shrug and carries on into the schoolyard. My eyes follow his black hoodie with disgust. "Urgh. What a loser."

"I know, right," Laura agrees. "Why the hell they let

someone from the Racecourse in, God alone only knows."

So, I'd better explain a bit here, I guess. My assailant was Jack Ryman, the school's resident goth. When he deigns to talk to anyone else, he says that his rejection of school uniform for the obsidian monochrome is a protest against conformity and brainwashing. However, we *all* know it's *really* because he's poor and can't afford decent clothes. He lives over on the Racecourse Estate. Apparently, it used to be full of things called *council houses*, which sound like they were utterly dreadful — small pokey things where they threw the scum of the town. Sort of like a mini Australia, you know what I mean? Anyway, most people on the estate own their own houses now rather than, Heaven forbid, rent them. But it's not somewhere that *I'd* want to go, no way. Full of druggies and pimps. God knows why anyone would want to live there.

We have no idea how Jack managed to get into our school. He must have passed the entrance exam, we all did, but God knows how. Must've cheated, somehow. I mean, let's face it, poor people aren't clever, are they? That's why they're poor.

I love school.

Now, I know what you're going to say, that it's *boring* and there's all those *lessons* and awful *teachers*, but I reckon it's what you make of it. Let's face it, people died so that we could go to school. In the war and stuff. So, we really ought to be grateful. Plus, all my friends are there. Sure, there's Physics (yuk), but there's also Art and P.E., both of which I'm really good at. I reckon, when I leave school, I'll set up my own art studio. It's going to be so popular. I'll spend all day painting and showing my work to everyone who comes in. I'll have such fun and it'll make me a fortune.

Which will be really useful when Mike and I have kids, obviously.

I reckon we'll have two. A boy and a girl, of course. I know I'm an only one and it's great having all the attention of my parents but sometimes I just think… you know. It would be nice to have someone there who's my age. I'll be sitting in my room, doing something, and I'll find myself turning to tell my brother (not sure why I see them as a brother) about what I'm doing. But he's not there, obviously. It's weird.

Not the sort of thing I tell my friends, that's for sure.

Like the nightmares.

Some things are best kept to yourself.

Let's face it. You don't want the men in white coats carting you off to the loony bin. Especially when you have a life as good as mine.

Anyway, enough of that. I was saying about how great school is. I just love it! On the whole, everyone's really friendly. Well, everyone who matters, anyway. At lunchtimes, a select group of us meet up under the trees behind the netball courts. There's this nice bench that isn't all skanky and wobbly and it's always free for us. Well, almost always. Sometimes you get some rando Year Eights there, but Mike sees them off, the little squirts. So, we chill out there, and talk about the deep stuff, you know.

"Have you seen this week's *Love Island*?"

"What do you think Kim and Kourtney will be up to this week?"

"Do you think that spot on Mister Milliband's nose is cancer? I bet it is."

But this lunchtime, there was only one topic of conversation. At assembly, Sachs, the deputy head, had announced something devastating.

"I can't believe it," says Laura.

"Me neither," agrees Maisie Preston. (She's nice. She's got this lovely handbag I'm really jealous of, but she doesn't ram it in your face, you know?) "It's so unfair."

The others around the bench nod.

"What were we talking about?" Mike asks, looking up from his phone.

Eight pairs of eyes (mine included) turn to my boyfriend. "The *Kidsweek* disco tomorrow."

His face brightens and those gorgeous blues sparkle in the late March sunshine. "Yeah, it's cool. I'm really looking forward to it. My dad's bought me this awesome tux..." His voice trails off as the sighing starts around our circle of friends.

Laura looks at me and raises an eyebrow.

I chew my lip the way I do when I get nervous and I lay my hand on Mike's. "Seriously, Baby, you do need to pay more attention when others are talking about important stuff, you know?"

"Like when Petty tells me I need to plough down the pitch and take out anyone who stands in my way."

I nod enthusiastically. "That's right. That's exactly it." Keeping my hand on his, I explain, "You won't be able to wear your tux tomorrow. Do you remember Sachs saying they'd banned our own clothes and we've got to go in uniform?"

Mike frowns. I can see him desperately trying to recall the deputy head's voice in assembly. Eventually, he shakes his head.

I sigh. "It's because those idiots ran through town

last night causing chaos. They smashed up quite a bit of stuff and the police are actually involved. So, the Head wants to make a point that we have to be respectable. As a result, school uniform."

"Oh." Mike's eyes narrow. "But my tux isn't uniform. How am I supposed to wear it?"

A groan rises from the other side of the bench. It's Pete Harvey. To be honest, I'm not sure why he hangs with us. He likes the sound of his voice too much. Probably because his dad's on the local council.

"What?" I snap at Pete.

"Seriously Mandy? Can't you get him upgraded or something? He runs slower than a tortoise on a Nokia."

"Shut up, Pete," I grumble.

Like I said, Pete likes the sound of his own voice. As a result, he doesn't know when to stop.

"I mean, Goliath here might be great on the rugby pitch, but what the hell do you really see in him? He's hardly the conversationist."

I grip my hands tight and feel my nails dig into my palms.

Pete either doesn't notice my anger or just chooses to ignore it. He's on a roll.

"Remember that time he thought a lasagna was a fancy Italian sports car? Jesus!"

At the back of my head, I'm walking up the stairway again, holding the candle. Its flame is getting brighter and brighter.

"And what about last mufti day when he thought we had to bring in a muffin." Pete laughs out loud and a tear rolls down his cheek.

The candle in my head flares.

Pete jumps up from where he's sitting and swears

loudly as he smacks the back of his left hand with his right. "Jesus! Ow! Jesus!"

I blink and I'm back in the here and now — no creepy staircase; no burning candle.

What the hell just happened?

Pete is whingeing and whimpering as he gathers up his stuff so that he can head off to the school nurse and get her to check over the burn on the back of his hand. The bell goes, signalling the end of lunch and the rest of us drift back to our lessons.

The others are talking about what the afternoon holds in store for them.

In the back of my head, I feel my bare feet walking up a crumbling stone staircase.

Chapter Two

Mike's busy after school. It's a Friday so he has Rugby practice. Normally, I'd stay and watch. It's great watching him charge up and down the pitch. Laura normally comes along and sits with me. We always cheer and clap when he scores a try. I'm not sure why they call it that when they score. Let's face it, they've done more than just try; they've succeeded.

Anyway, Laura and I cheer him on, even if we don't fully understand the game.

I decided that I'd go straight home tonight. I told Mike and he asked me if we'd be meeting up later.

Mike and I have this really romantic thing going on where he waits around the corner from my house and I sneak out my bedroom window on Friday nights. Don't look at me like that. It's nothing sordid and we're not out mugging grannies or vandalising stuff. It's just our little thing. We get to have a bit of quiet time once a week when it's just us. Only an hour or so, then I creep back in and go to bed.

You see, if I have one criticism about my parents, it's that they are a tad overprotective. I didn't mind when I was a little kid, but as I started to grow up, I guess I kicked back a bit. As a result, I started to sneak out at night. The thing was, it wasn't really that interesting. I'd just wander around Sale, where I live, and get bored.

That was until Mike and his family moved here last year. We just clicked, you know? So now, once a week, I keep up the sneaking out, but we use it for our quality time together.

But not tonight. I told him that I was really tired and would be having an early night before getting ready for the disco tomorrow.

He nodded and bounded off to practice like a happy puppy.

He's such a sweetie.

I hate lying to him.

To be honest, I am tired, but it's more down to what happened at lunch with Pete. Perhaps I *did* burn him? Let's face it, I was having some sort of weird flashback to that dream. It has to be connected, right?

Fortunately, Laura knows nothing about my dreams. Like I said before, I've not told anyone. So, as we're walking out the school drive, she's chatting away about what she's up to tonight and how I ought to Face-Time her after tea so we can discuss makeup for tomorrow. "They may not be letting us wear our dresses," she says, "but they can't stop us from looking fabulous."

I actually laugh at this. Laura really is a good friend and I reckon she knows I'm feeling out of sorts, even if she doesn't know why, so she's doing her best to cheer me up.

I've just about forgotten about the incident at lunchtime when I feel a shove to my back and I almost fall to the floor.

"What the hell?" I yell, turning around.

And, just like that, it all comes flooding back. Pete's standing there, waving a bandaged hand in my face. "Look what you did!" he screams at me. "Look what you did, Mandy! I know it was you! You were angry and you were looking at me all weird."

"For God's sake, Pete," Laura snaps. "What on Earth are you going on about? Don't you know how stupid you sound?"

He rounds on my friend. "Stupid? You think my hand just catching fire is stupid?" It's now Laura's turn to have the bandage waved in her face. "It hurt like a bitch."

Give Laura her due, she doesn't back down in the face of his anger. Stepping up to him, she jabs the back of the bandage with a finger, making Pete wince. "Oh, and Mandy just miraculously fluttered her eyelids and you burst into flame? Get real! You probably rubbed it against the bench and gave yourself a friction burn."

"Does this look like a friction burn? Does it?" Pete pushes past my defender and squares up with me. I'm starting to feel really frightened now. He's always had a mouth on him, but I've never seen him act like this. "Admit it, Mandy, you're a freak. *You* did this to me."

The pupils from school are giving the three of us a very wide berth as Pete reaches out with his good hand and grabs hold of my shoulder. I cry out and try to break free but he's holding on incredibly tight.

Then suddenly, there's a blur and Pete's hand is no longer on my shoulder. What's more, Pete's feet aren't touching the ground either. This is because he's being held up in the air at arm's length by the Creep.

I look across at Laura and she's just standing there, her mouth open wide.

Pete is batting with his hands (one bandaged, one not) at the gloved hand that is holding him by his shirt front. The dark glasses of the Creep turn from Pete to me then back up again.

"You do not touch her."

His voice is not what I had expected. I guess, I thought he would be all rough and gnarly, like how he looks. But it was deep and weirdly sophisticated.

"You do not touch her," the Creep repeats. With his free hand, he grabs Pete's bandage and squeezes. It must really hurt as Pete cries like a baby. Not only that but he pisses himself. Laura looks away in embarrassment but I just stand staring at what's going on in front of me.

What the hell is happening to my life?

The Creep releases his grip and drops Pete into the pool of piss that the boy has made. Like lightning, his foot is suddenly on Pete's chest and Pete is screaming for him to let go. The Creep bends low and his dark glasses stare into Pete's face. Pete falls deathly silent and just nods. The Creep removes his foot and turns to face me.

Needless to say, I take a few steps backwards.

I watch his shoulders rise and fall, as if he's sighing, and then he does something weird.

Well, something *weirder*.

He lifts his head and looks like he's sniffing at the air. His dark glasses seem to shoot off down Marsland Road and, after giving me a quick look, he wanders off down the street.

Laura steps around Pete, who is lying curled up on the floor, whimpering to himself. "You okay?" she asks.

I shrug. "Let's go. People are watching."

So we head off.

I don't tell Mum or Dad about what happened after school. I mean, would *you*? They'd freak. I know they would. Like I explained earlier, they're rather overprotective. When I was little, they'd never let me do anything dangerous. I was never allowed to climb trees (not that I ever really wanted to) or join any club that might get me hurt, such as karate. The plus side was that I never broke any bones or stuff like that. I never really got ill, either. I guess that not mixing in close contact with lots of groups of different kids meant that I didn't pick up all the random germs that circulate all the time.

Still, I needed something physical to do. So, I took up running.

I love it. It's a time when I can just tune everything out and enjoy my own company. I love my family and my friends, but there are those times when I just want to be on my own. I'm sure you know what I mean. We all have a need for solitude, don't we? Being popular can be so tiring.

Anyway, after tea, I get changed, stick my earbuds in and head out for a run. I don't go far, just down Moss Lane, along Harboro Road and back up Hillington before home. Enough of a distance to work up a sweat and clear my head.

When I get home, I strip off and climb into a wonderfully hot bath that's full of bubbles.

Bliss.

All the stresses and strains of the day immediately soak away. There's some chill music playing on my speaker, I've got the lights turned down low and there's even some candles that I've lit.

Basically, It's perfection.

Until I start to drift off, that is.

As the sweet scent of the candle reaches my nose, I let my eyes droop shut and I feel myself drifting away. It's warm. Very warm. I'm walking through dry, dusty streets. There are so many people around me. It's even busier than the city centre at Christmas. People are all crowded together and there's a stink of big fat cows pulling wooden carts. There are houses around me and they're small and tatty but, weirdly, the people all seem happy. They occasionally call out and wave at me and my companion.

He's a small boy about my age (for some odd reason I'm about four or five in this dream — go figure) and he has dark brown hair and bright blue eyes.

Then it strikes me that we're the only white people in the town. All the others look like they're Indian or perhaps Pakistani. I'm not sure. What I do know, though, is that this is our home. This is where the two of us belong. We walk out of the huge town and into the countryside where a massive river flows past. We both giggle in that silly way that little children do and run up to the water's edge.

"Alec!" I cry out to the boy. "Look in the water." I reach out, placing my little hand in the river, and I giggle again. As I twirl my fingers around in lazy loops and whirls, the water starts to boil. "Look!" I cry out. "Look what I can do!"

Alec smiles then stares off into the distance as if he can hear a voice that I can't. "Mother is calling," he says. We straighten ourselves up, hold hands and walk back up to the city where a pretty woman is waiting for us. She has the same blue eyes as Alec and her long blonde hair is shot through with red streaks.

I awake with a gasp and curse as I leap out of what has turned into boiling-hot water. Grabbing a towel off the heated rail, I pat myself down, making sure that I've not been scalded. After a quick inspection and a few deep breaths, I pull the plug and let the water drain away.

Who the hell is the boy called Alec and who is the blonde woman?

I run my fingers down to my scalp where small roots of red are starting to poke through.

The woman with identical hair to me.

I don't know what to think. I mean, let's face it, what *should* I think? Seriously weird stuff is starting to happen. What should I do? Should I tell someone?

Who can I tell?

Before I go to sleep, I scroll through my phone to the *Let's Talk* website. I sit there for about five minutes before I pluck up the courage to type anything then I just ramble on about how things are all getting weird and I press *send*. Will I get a reply? I doubt it. Remember, she's not posted anything since January, so she's probably not reading her mails either.

But I had to say something to someone. If I don't, I'll burst.

I eventually drift off to sleep at some ungodly hour in the morning. As I feel myself finally get drowsy, I expect to have more weird dreams about the boy and my so-called mother, however, it's just the familiar walk up the familiar staircase with the familiar candle.

Just the same old, same old in Amanda's growing world of weird.

At least the morning brings Saturday, which means preparations for the *Kidsweek* disco. That, at least, should keep my mind occupied. What the hell can go crazy when you go to get your hair done and your nails pimped up?

So, let's get real for a moment, one of the best things about a big event is the prep. Sure, the event itself can be marvellous, but it's just over in a flash. *Poof!* and it's gone. But, the preparation and the *anticipation* of the big day… Well, that can take months or weeks. You have this little knot of buzziness bouncing around inside of you as the event gets ever closer and you have more and more things to do.

I'm a list girl. I don't do chaos. Not at all. Everything has to be planned and coordinated (normally in different coloured pens and highlighters) right down to the finest detail. Laura says that I'm a born bureaucrat, a micro-manager, and when I'm older I'll have my own office where I'll have thousands of slaves scurrying around under me as my spreadsheet automatically ticks off their tasks.

That would be rather cool…

As long as I have a fancy nameplate on my office door: "Amanda Harper: CEO and bureaucratic badass." Stop laughing. I know it's silly, but it's fun. I think I deserve a chuckle, what with all that dream craziness going on right now.

Anyway, my *TTD* list for the day of the disco is immense. Fortunately, Mother Harper is always more than happy to help out. So, together we burn through the tasks at hand like a mother and daughter crime-fighting duo. By about two in the afternoon, we arrive at what, for me, is the highlight of the multicoloured bullet list: the hairdressers.

We always go to the same salon. It's on the pedestrian precinct of School Road and is opposite Caffè Nero, so we can always send out for a nice coffee while my hair is being coloured. Normally, one of the girls from the salon nips over the road to grab them, but they are totally rushed off their feet, what with the *Kidsweek* disco event tonight, so Mum tells them not to worry and she heads over to grab our drinks.

I sit back and let the hairdresser get to work. It's a routine that I'm really used to as I have to come here on a regular basis to get my roots done.

So, yeah, I guess now would be a good time to explain about my hair.

Basically, I hate it.

I have it dyed blonde even though, like I said earlier, I'm a *natural* blonde. But blonde isn't the only colour that God decided to *bless* me with. For some crazy reason, he decided to dip a paintbrush in the red pot and splatter it on my head in random streaks.

I know, crazy right?

Those freak streaks used to get me called all sorts of names when I was little so, when I was old enough, I asked my mum if I could get them covered up. Being the angel that she is, of course she agreed. Hence, since I was about ten, we pop along here every few weeks to get that red painted over, obliterated and hidden away. Plus, it's nice to rock a new style every now and then. This time it's a sort of choppy side bob.

The regular routine has actually become part of our mother-and-daughter social calendar. Along with the coffee.

Talking of which, she seems to be taking her time.

I peer out of the window and I can see her standing outside of Caffè Nero holding two coffee cups. She looks like she's talking to a couple of people: one man and one woman. I don't recognise either of them. To be honest, I'm not sure that I would want to. They look what Laura would call, "*Real shady.*" The guy's hair is cut crazily close and he has a tattoo of a black dragon on the side of his neck. The woman is wearing something that looks like it's come straight off the peg from Primark in the city centre. They're not the sort of people that Mum would normally talk to. At first, I decide that she must be giving them directions or something, but the conversation seems to be going on far too long and looks like it's actually getting a bit heated. The guy is waving his hands around, as if he's trying to explain something. The woman is just standing there, her eyes staring straight at my mum.

My stomach is knotted up and I want to go to her, but my hair's still being done and I can't leave my seat.

Eventually, my mum nods, says something to the two randos and they leave. She turns to face the salon and walks over with the coffee.

"Here you go, Princess. A latte for you and a cappuccino for me. What's wrong?"

"Who were those two people you were talking to?"

"People?"

"In the street. Just now?"

Mum sips her coffee and winces. It's obviously still hot. "Oh, those two. Old school friends."

"Really?"

"Mmhmm. Not seen them in years."

I'm frowning. "They didn't seem very friendly."

"Well, to be quite honest, Princess, they weren't. Let's just say that they made some bad choices in life and they're the sort of folks that I wouldn't want to mix with these days."

I look up into her grey eyes. There's definitely worry

there. "You okay?"

She sips more coffee. "Absolutely fine. Have you decided what colour nails you're having?"

I decide on royal blue. The same colour as the dress that I wasn't allowed to wear.

So, I guess you know what *Kidsweek* is all about. Let's face it, it's impossible to miss every year. But I suppose some people do live under a rock, so I'd better summarise, just in case. Every year lots of celebrities get together and, at the end of March, put on a heartfelt television extravaganza to remind us that there are those out there who are less fortunate than us. They film videos of themselves going places that look absolutely dreadful: Africa, India, Wolverhampton. The poverty is unbelievable! All these poor people live in such tiny little houses and the celebrities talk about how they don't have enough money to make ends meet. It must be dreadful. I reckon they probably only get to go on one big holiday a year.

It's probably not even abroad.

Mind you, that's not really an issue for those living in other countries. They're already abroad, I guess. So, at least it's already sunny for them.

Laura's very dismissive of the whole thing. She says that her dad says (he's got a job in the financial district in the city) that it's because they've all got too many kids. Her dad says that if they weren't allowed to breed then the world would be much better off.

Personally, I think that's rather harsh, so I don't say anything back when she gets on her high horse and gallops around the place on that one. She's my friend and I don't want to upset her.

As I get ready to go out on Saturday evening, I've

got a *Kidsweek* video streaming in my room. They stick loads on YouTube in the week before. I guess it's to help you get in the mood or something.

Well, it's certainly affecting my mood.

The presenter is walking around this little village somewhere hot and all the children are running after him, smiling and shouting. As they do, I feel odd inside. The dream that I had in the bath starts to creep back into my mind and I hear the sounds of the people from it over the top of these children. For a moment, it's as if I'm in two places at once. My head starts to spin and I feel myself swaying.

I quickly sit down on the edge of my bed and close my eyes, breathing slowly. I run my fingers over the soft floral duvet. Yes. This is where I am. Not somewhere where there's no running water, no internet connection and no proper toilets.

The spinning subsides and I open my eyes.

In the video, the presenter is talking to a woman whose daughter died from cholera.

It's good that we're having the disco. These people really need our money.

My mobile buzzes. It's Mike. He's waiting outside in the limo.

It's rather weird walking into the school hall on Mike's arm this evening. Oh, not the being with Mike bit. No, that's *perfect*. No, what I mean is seeing everyone in their school uniform. The absolute highlight of the annual *Kidsweek* disco is the outfits. You have all the boys standing around in their tuxes, looking terribly handsome, and all the girls are in their dresses, some pulling it off better than others.

This year, we all just look… well… the same. It's one big mass of black and white. But, we have to look on the bright side. At least we're still *having* the disco. Imagine if they'd cancelled it!

Imagine the outcry from the pupils at being deprived of such a wonderful social occasion.

So, Mike and I are wandering through the hall saying *hi* to everyone. He high-fives all his rugby crew and Laura scooches up, dragging along her date for the evening (a boy in her geography set). We tell each other how pretty we look and admire each other's nails and hair. She compliments my new cut and I tell her how jealous I am of her long braids.

The usual.

Then I hear a voice behind me that seriously turns my stomach.

"Hey, Mandy. How's things?"

My eyes take a quick journey up into their sockets and back down before I turn around. "Hey, Georgia. I'm fine, thanks. You look…" I eye up her scarlet lipstick. So overdone. "Nice."

"Thanks, babe." She turns to Mike. "Hey, Mister Hunk." Jesus, can she thrust her chest out any further? Her blouse is going to burst. "You're smelling great tonight." She gets up close and, dear God, actually sniffs him. I want to vomit.

"Just my usual," Mike explains. "I know Mandy likes it."

I sigh. "So, who are you with *tonight*?"

Georgia switches her attention back to me. "*Will's* around here *somewhere*. I'll go and find him later."

I'm about to say something that I'll probably regret when the music starts up. I grab Mike by the hand, mutter a vague goodbye at the school slut and drag *my* man over onto the dance floor. It's an upbeat number to start the evening and soon all thoughts of Georgia Brandscombe and her heaving cleavage are drifting out of my mind.

This is great! I've been looking forward to this for months. It's totally what I need. This is the sort of life that I should be living, not worrying about creepy dreams. It's awesome to actually be here and letting my hair down.

Especially with Mike.

Every now and then, they put a slower number on and we dance close. I let his arms and his aftershave envelop me. It's paradise. I couldn't wish for a better evening.

Even without my dress.

It's about an hour in and I'm having a blast. However, I'm also thirsty, so I leave Mike grooving on the dance floor with his rugby crew and go to grab a drink. One of the home economics teachers ladles out a tumbler of their definitely non-alcoholic punch and I drink it gratefully. As I drop the cup in the recycling bin I see a black-clad figure lurking at the edge of the hall.

"Didn't expect to see you here. I didn't think it'd be your sort of thing."

Jack Ryman turns from studying the rest of the school enjoying themselves and shrugs. "Got to be somewhere, I suppose. Might as well come and support the big capitalist screw over."

"And what's that supposed to mean?"

He snorts in apparent amusement. "Trust me. You wouldn't understand. But then, you understand very little."

For a moment, I'm stunned into silence but then I let rip. "How dare you! Are you suggesting I'm thick or

something? I'll let you know I'm doing very well in my subjects."

"Really?"

"Yes, really!"

"It's art and P.E., isn't it? The *subjects* you took as
your options?"

"What of it?"

"Well, you're hardly going to be a merchant banker
just by running around a field or drawing an apple."

I can feel my blood beginning to boil. The palms of
my hands are starting to tingle. "But, that's not what I want
in life. I'm going to open an art studio and I'm going to
marry Mike. We're going to have two kids: a boy and a
girl. It'll be perfect."

Jack raises an eyebrow. "Perfect?"

I nod.

"Well, you'd better tell that to Georgia, then." He
turns around and walks away laughing.

Frowning, I turn to look out across the dance floor
and my world revolves upside down.

Georgia Brandscome has her arms around Mike's
neck and she's snogging him! That slut's tart red lips are
locked onto the mouth of my future husband! How? How
can this be happening to me?

I cry out in anger and storm out of the hall, out of
the school, my cheeks flushed scarlet.

Tears are streaming from my eyes and I'm rubbing
angrily at them as I run down the drive to the road. My
head is full of what I've just witnessed and I don't realise
there's someone behind me until a firm hand grabs my
shoulder.

Chapter Three

Oh God, oh God, oh God! What's happening?

Someone's clasped a hand over my mouth and there's an arm around my middle. My own arms are pinned to my sides as I feel my whole body lurch sideways. I'm kicking frantically as I'm dragged along the street. I'm screaming for all it's worth against my attacker's hand, but I don't think I'm making much noise as they're successfully muffling me.

I'm being manhandled around the corner to Beaufort Road and my eyes widen as I see a large black van parked on the double yellows, its back door open like a hungry monstrous mouth. I start to struggle frantically and my abductor's grip tightens. They hiss in annoyance and pick up speed towards the van.

I can't let them get me in there. I can't!

They heave me up and I twist in their arms. Placing my foot on the step up into the back of the van, I push backwards as hard as I can. There's a rough grunting and we both tumble backwards. My attacker cries out. It's a harsh male voice. His grip slackens as he hits the floor and I tumble out of his arms. Without thinking, I roll to my feet and begin to run.

I dart back around the corner without looking back and instinctively head over Marsland Road towards the safety of school.

There are people there.

It will be safe.

I can raise the alarm.

Darting across the pedestrian crossing, I collide with a black shape and I scream.

"Whoa! Mandy! You okay?"

My face turns up to the source of the voice. It's Jack Ryman. He looks seriously worried.

"Jack! Jack! You've got to help me."

"I know. I saw you run out. I thought I'd better check on you."

I shake my head. "No. Not that. Someone just tried to kidnap me. They tried to get me into a van!"

His forehead creases. "What? Seriously? Surely…"

"Please!" I hear my voice rise in panic. "Please. Get me inside. We need to tell someone."

He glances over my shoulder and frowns. "But, there's no one there."

I snatch a look back out at the street. He's right. There's no sign of anyone. "They were there," I insist.

Jack stares into my face, his brow still furrowed, then nods. "Come on. Let's get inside."

We turn and start to head down the school drive. As we pass through the gates, a figure steps out of the shadows. "Mandy?" calls out a familiar voice.

Right now, all my anger and revulsion at Georgia throwing herself at my boyfriend is something from another life. I run from Jack to Mike and throw myself into the arms of my strong, rugby-playing man. I start to cry.

"It's okay," he says, stroking my hair. "It's okay."

I can hear Jack saying that we need to find an adult. He's telling Mike about what happened.

Mike just continues to stroke my hair, the strong, familiar scent of his aftershave wafting over me.

Jack's voice is rising. He sounds annoyed that Mike is ignoring him. He repeats that we need to find a teacher or someone.

Still, Mike ignores him. I am his entire world and he is mine. All past sins are forgiven.

Jack says that he's going to go and get an adult and I hear his shoes crunch against the rough asphalt.

I hear another sound, too.

It sounds like a boot being drawn out of wet, sticky mud. It's followed by another noise I've never heard before and I can't describe. I pull away from Mike's tender embrace and turn to see a sight that just can't be possible.

My boyfriend's right arm is much longer than it should be and it's impaled through Jack's chest. Jack is staring blankly down at the impossible thing in his body, his jaw juddering up and down, drool pouring over his chin. He coughs and blood erupts from his mouth. Mike jerks his arm backwards and Jack collapses on the school driveway — a pile of flesh and bones clothed in black. Blood is pooling from the wounds in his chest and his back.

I stare, stupefied, at Mike's arm.

There's no hand! There's no hand!

It's... it's a long spike and it's covered in blood. Jack's blood!

He... he... killed Jack. There in front of me. He changed his arm into a long spike and he shoved it through Jack's chest.

Jack's dead. There in front of me. He's lying on the floor, dead. He's not going to move again.

He's dead.

Mike… Mike… is a monster.

I scream. Oh, I scream so loudly. And I run. I don't know where I'm running to. I just run as fast as I can to get away from this monster. I'm aware of the school building looming up in front of me as panic consumes me. All I can think of is finding someone. Someone to save me from this monster.

Then, in a flash, the floor rises to meet me. Something has snaked around my ankle and caused me to trip over. I hit the ground hard and all the wind leaves my lungs. I wriggle over onto my back and stare in disbelief at Mike's too-long arm wrapped around my ankle as he reels me in over the school driveway.

He's going to kill me!

He's going to do to me what he did to Jack.

But then there's a blur and his grip slackens as he cries out in agony.

It's… it's the Creep… He's got a long knife in his gloved hand. He's chopped it through Mike's repulsive arm, cutting it in two. He glances quickly at me through his dark glasses before pulling the bandages away from his mouth. Then he's a blur again and Mike screams even louder. The Creep has thrust the knife up into my monster boyfriend's chest. He then rams his face into Mike's neck and Mike struggles desperately to free himself. As he turns and twists in the Creep's clutches, his body seems to warp and twist, as if it's not solid.

But his attempts to escape become rapidly weaker.

After a short while, the Creep pulls back and Mike

falls to the floor. As he does, my boyfriend disintegrates into dust.

Freaking dust!!!

What the hell is happening here?

The Creep turns towards me, slides his knife into his coat somewhere and holds out his gloved hands, palms facing outwards. "Are you okay?" comes the muffled but polite voice. "Are you hurt?"

I can't take any more of this. I… just… can't…

I crawl over onto all fours then launch myself up and forwards towards the school door.

The Creep's standing in front of me, between me and the building! How did he do that? How can he move so fast?

"Please… Please…" My head is shaking. Tears are streaming down my cheeks.

The Creep takes a step forward.

I spin around and make to run.

There's a warm pressure around my throat. I can smell stale, unwashed clothing.

I can't even begin to struggle as spots form in my vision and everything greys.

Then, all is black.

It's cold. So very cold.

I light a match and the flare from its tip gives a small amount of illumination to the gloom. I lower the flame to the tip of the candle that rests on the low stone wall next to me before dropping the match, discarded, on the damp grass.

As I pick up the small candle by its brass holder, I hear movement behind me. Slowly, so as not to extinguish the flame that gutters and dances in the wind, I turn in an attempt to locate the source of the noise. It's dark, incredibly dark, and hard to make out what's lurking in the gloom behind me, but I am sure that I can see movement in the deep shadows.

I call out but the wind snatches my voice away into the night.

I hear the sound again.

It is familiar.

It is deadly.

It is one I have heard before: like a boot being drawn out of wet mud.

Cautiously, I edge backwards, one hand holding my candle, the other steadying myself against the low stone wall. My heart is pounding and my stomach is rolling as the creatures begin to loom out of the dark. They are tall, broad and have no face. Their skin looks like wet dirt and they possess long arms that reach down beneath their knees.

But it's not their appearance that chills me most. It is the sound of their uniform marching.

Thud, thud.

Thud, thud.

Thud, thud.

Unstoppable. Relentless. Soulless.

And they are coming for me.

"Come to me. Come to me, my child…"

The male voice carries across the wind and I turn around to see from where it has come. There is an old tower at the end of the wall, an archway at its base. I run towards it, desperate to escape the marching monsters that have come for me. I grip the candleholder tightly. I must not drop it as the insides of the tower are pitch black and I do not want to stumble up its spiralling staircase. My bare feet slap against the old stone stairs as I climb upwards, upwards. The tower begins to shake and shudder. Not only is the wind buffeting its sides, but the creatures have begun to climb, single file, up the narrow staircase.

The stairs shake beneath me and I grab frantically at the crumbling wall as I hurry upwards.

I *cannot* let them catch me.

I *must not* let them catch me.

"Come to me. Come to me, my child…" the voice calls out once again and I increase my speed.

Eventually, after what feels to be an eternity, I am standing at the top of the spiral staircase. In front of me is a familiar wooden door. I have seen this door so many times. I can identify every knot and pattern on its ancient surface. Frantically, I run my hand over the battered surface in a vain attempt to locate a handle, but there is none.

Thud, thud.

Thud, thud.

Thud, thud.

The pounding rhythm of ascending feet is getting closer and I start to hit at the door with my fist, screaming into the howling wind that whips through the open windows of the tower.

Noises carry on the wind and reach my ears, causing me to turn and glance out of the window.

What I see scares me even more than the monsters that are now almost upon me.

There, on a bleak hillside, are two dragons, one black and one red with seven heads. They are fighting and, as each of them swipes at their respective opponent, their cruel talons gouge into rough, scaly skin, causing fire and blood to rain down on the land below.

"Amanda, come!" the voice urges. It's coming from behind the door and I shake my head. There's no way to open the door. I am stranded here in a tower that feels like it's going to collapse as faceless monsters reach out to grab me and dragons destroy the world below them in their battle.

It's hopeless.

"It's never hopeless. I have faith in you."

I swallow it all down, all the fear, the nerves, the panic, and I feel it swirling around inside my stomach, brewing and boiling into something different. I place my hand on the door, at the spot where there should be a handle, and I scream in frustration, in anger and in sheer bloody-mindedness.

And something miraculous happens.

My hand bursts into flame.

As I feel the monsters reach the upper steps behind me, I push my fiery hand against the wood and the door ignites. Fingers of fire skitter across its surface and the wood crumbles away to ash, leaving a fiery portal in its place.

I step through.

On the other side stands a man. He is relatively tall, has dark hair and wears a denim jacket that seems to have two badges pinned to it. He lowers the dark glasses that he's wearing and his eyes are pure fire.

"That's my girl," he says.

I awake with a gasp.

It's cold. Very cold. I'm actually shivering as I wake up. I move my arms to wrap them around me even before I open my eyes, which I do slowly. Running my frozen hands up and down my arms that still wear my school shirt, I take in the room in which I'm lying, curled up on my side. It's dark but I can make out certain things. The first is the smell. It's damp and dusty, like the place hasn't been used in a long time. The dust actually makes my nose twitch but I force back a reflexive sneeze as I let my eyes wander as best they can.

The floor upon which I'm lying is wooden. It looks rough and splintered. I can feel the splinters digging into my cheek. The rest of the room is mostly empty. There looks to be some rubbish over on the far side: some boxes, a pile of old metal or machinery and other stuff. From where I lie, the room seems to be quite large. My guess is that it's some sort of warehouse or old factory that has been cleared out.

Not somewhere that people will come looking for me.

Am I going to die here?

I feel a tear start to edge its way out of my right eye.

There's the sound of movement beyond the field of my vision.

"Are you awake?" comes a familiar, reserved voice.

I close my eyes down to a thin squint that allows me to appear asleep but lets me see a small bit.

The floorboards creak.

"Her heartbeat has raised a touch, which suggests that she is awake. There. Her pulse is quickening. She must be able to hear me. Do you think I hurt her? I didn't mean to hurt her."

The voice is definitely that of the Creep, but who is he talking to? I can't see well enough and I can't hear anyone else. There's no sound of any other movement or anyone else's footsteps.

"I had no choice. I had no choice. She was scared

and struggling and constructs were there. I couldn't let them harm her. I had to act quickly."

Silence.

"I know. I know. I panicked. I panicked." The Creep begins to pace the room. As he does, he passes my barely open eyes and I see his tattered trousers and dirty shoes walk in front of me. Small eddies of dust plume up from the floor in his wake. "It's so hard without you."

Well, that's weird.

He paces a bit more before stopping in front of me. He crouches down in front of me. "Amanda, I know you're awake. There's no point trying to hide it. Please, can we talk?"

I don't want to talk.

I don't want to be here with this psycho!

Suddenly, I push my arms out and connect my hands with the floor. Shoving up, I propel myself forward and attempt to run past him like a sprinter launching from their blocks, but my legs give out and I tumble over. I cry out in pain as I crash to the floor.

"No, no, no!" the Creep cries out and I feel him beside me, his gloved hands running over my blouse. "Please, don't. You'll hurt yourself."

"Get away from me!" I scream as I try to tear myself away from him. I dig my nails into the wooden floorboards and scratch my way across the floor, willing my legs to work. "Get away!" I scream again. A hand lowers onto my shoulder and I shriek. He's crazy! He's going to kill me. I have to escape.

"She's distressed! What should I do? What would *you* do?"

My head snaps left and right. There's no one else in the room. It's just me and this schizo! I'm going to be brutally raped and murdered if I don't get away. I have to escape.

The same feelings from my dream of panic and dread are churning around in my stomach as I try to scrabble myself away from the Creep. I feel them boiling and bubbling inside of me, starting to form something else. Sweat breaks out on the nape of my neck and my hands suddenly feel incredibly hot. I roll over onto my back and see him bending over me in that disgusting coat of his, wearing those stupid rags across his face.

And I hate him! I completely and utterly hate him.

As the savage emotion overwhelms me, my hands burst into flame.

Two things now happen simultaneously: the Creep takes a step back in obvious fear and I faint.

Something is different now. I've woken up again after what has possibly been the most peaceful sleep I've had in months. There has been no tower, no staircase, no candle or a door without a handle. I haven't been chased by faceless monsters or watched dragons fighting.

Instead, I feel like I've been lying in a comfortable bed and someone has been gently holding my hand, whispering into my ear that everything will be alright.

That's not the only thing. I'm warmer now. Not much, but enough to stop me from shivering. There's a rough blanket draped over me. It smells awful, but I draw it closer as I wake up.

"I'm sorry," ventures a small voice from the other side of the room.

I pull myself up to a sitting position. I am still in the same place. It is lighter now as rays of sunlight are break-ing into the gloom. I can see them lancing through holes in the roof and through gaps between a pair of large doors at the other end of the room.

Doors.

Doors through which I can escape.

I tense and relax my legs. They feel like they're responding better now. I could make a break for it, but would it be successful? I don't know if the doors are locked or not. Plus, I've seen how fast the Creep can move.

Plus…

Plus, there's something else. I recall the sensation of someone holding my hand during my sleep as they comforted me.

"Who are you?"

The Creep is sitting with his back to a wall, his long legs curled up in front of him. "My name is Marcus. I am here to protect you."

"Great job you're doing there," I snap.

The Creep starts to hit the back of his head against the wall behind him. Loose plaster showers down onto his dirty rags. "She hates me! She hates me!" he wails. "I'm failing! I'm failing! What should I do?"

What the hell is going on here?

"Stop that!" I call out across his rambling.

He immediately does as I say and I wince as I rearrange my position.

"Are you going to hurt me?"

His dark glasses lock onto me. There's no expression that I can see through his bandaged face, but I instinctively know that under those tattered, dirty rags, there's a look of utter horror. "No! Never! You are one of the Twins. It is my purpose to protect you."

"I'm not a twin. I don't have a brother."

My captor's head twitches to one side. "Yet, your heart just skipped. Plus, you specifically said, *brother*. Have you seen him? In your dreams, perhaps?"

I remain silent.

The Creep nods. "What else have you seen, Amanda?"

I can feel my anger begin to rise again and I thrust my hands down under the stinking blanket. "Don't talk to me as if you know me. You don't know me!"

"No, I don't," the Creep sighs. "Not personally, at least. But I know *of* you. All my kind do. We were instructed to protect you by the one who created us."

Created? "What do you mean? Are you a monster like Mike was?"

A sharp tutting noise escapes the Creep's rags. "He was a construct; a creature of clay sent back in time by Kanor, the one who will destroy all that you hold dear."

And… suddenly we're back visiting Crazy Town.

"You seem to be having a hard time accepting all this."

"No… No… It's all good. Just the other day, I was chatting to the Easter Bunny about how Father Christmas was going to visit me this year if I was a good girl."

"I can tell you're upset."

"Seriously? You think?"

"I do, and I understand. I understand completely. I… What is the term you youngsters use these days? Yes, that's it. I *freaked out* somewhat when I was introduced to this world. When I was turned into what I am now."

"What's that then? A crazy kidnapper?"

I don't even see him move. One second, he's sitting over on the other side of the room; the next he's up close in my face.

"No, Amanda. I'm a vampire."

It's safe to say that I am now screaming my head off. I'm pushing myself as far back from him as possible but the wall behind me is preventing me from getting away from this monster.

A vampire! A freaking vampire! I want to deny it, to say it's not possible, but after the things I've just been through…

I realise that he's talking, his voice low and soothing. His gloved hands are stretched out towards me in a placating gesture and he scooches back a bit, giving me space. "It's okay. I'm not going to hurt you. I'm not here to hurt you. I'm here to protect you."

"Then, why would you say you're a vampire?"

"Because that is what I am."

"You're nuts! Vampires aren't real!"

"You saw what I did to the construct before?"

The image of Mike turning to dust as the Creep latched onto his neck revisits my memory and I shudder. I nod.

"We were created to fight the constructs, to search through history for you and your twin brother."

"Why?"

He pauses. "We don't know."

I can't stop myself. I actually laugh. "Seriously? Some guy gives you a task to do and you don't know what for? What else did he tell you to do? Concoct the perfect lasagna?"

"Find the Eternals; Protect the Twins; Await the Divergence."

I frown. "What the hell does all that mean?"

The Creep's head turns to the side and he says, "She is obviously confused. She wants answers."

"Who are you talking to?"

The dark glasses turn back and focus on me. He tugs nervously at one glove with another before manoeuvring himself into a crossed-leg position in front of me. "I recently lost someone very dear to me. She had been my companion for many, many years. I'm just not used to her not being here."

His voice sounds sad, haunted.

"I'm sorry. Did you love her?"

I can't see his mouth, but I am sure there's a touch of a smile behind those rags. "Not romantically," he explains.

"What was her name?"

"Nightingale."

"That's a pretty name."

"I know. It suited her. She didn't deserve to die."

"How did she die?"

For a moment, it's like I'm sitting staring at the weirdest statue ever. He is completely motionless: a bunch of filthy clothes and rags in human form. Then he seems to sigh and says, "Someone exposed her to sunlight. She burned to death."

My hand jumps to my mouth in shock.

My hand.

I stare at my fingers and recall his terror when they burst into flame. He stares at them too and nods.

"It's as easy as that. If you want to run, to escape, all you have to do is conjure up that fire again and let it loose on me. I won't stop you."

I look from my hand to the swaddled face. A face which I cannot see, the emotions of its wearer that I cannot truly read. Yet, I believe him. Don't ask me why. I just do.

"I won't hurt you," I promise. "As long as you don't try to hurt me. After all, you did save my life."

He nods.

What now? I'm stuck in an abandoned warehouse with a sort of crazy vampire who thinks he has to protect me. My boyfriend was a weird monster and I have fire superpowers.

"You have questions."

"Lots, I guess."

"Where would you like to begin?"

I glance back at my hand. "What am I? Why could I do that?"

"We are not sure. All we know is that we have to protect you and your brother."

"You were right. I saw him in a dream. We were little kids. Our mother was there, too. She had my hair and his eyes: blonde and blue." Then something strikes me. "Wait. If the woman in my dream is my mother, then who are my parents?"

"They are like your boyfriend. They are constructs."

I shake my head. "No. No. They can't be. They love me. They care for me. They've certainly never gone all…" I stretch my arms out and wave them around in a stabby fashion.

"It is possible that they don't even know. The planet's population has been seeded with thousands of constructs that live everyday lives until they are triggered for a specific purpose or until the day of the Divergence."

"You mentioned that before. What is it?"

"The day that Kanor rises. The day he will waken his construct army and decimate humanity."

Well, that certainly sucks!

"Are these eternal things you're looking for something to do with it?"

"They are the Cup and the Blade. They have exis-ted from the beginning of time itself."

"And their purpose is?"

He is ominously quiet.

"You don't know, do you?"

"We were instructed to find them by our creator."

I sit back against the wall and cross my arms. "It seems to me that you've taken a lot of what you were told to do purely on faith. Don't you wonder *why* you were given these tasks?"

"They have been our purpose for millennia."

"Yet, you've never questioned them?"

"Why should we?"

I laugh out loud. "Seriously? What if the guy who created you was an utter psycho? What if he's using you for, I don't know... *nefarious reasons*?"

The Creep shakes his head. "No, we are the Chil-dren of Cain. We have walked in the shadows of history, watching over humanity and fulfilling our tasks. We..."

"Whoa, whoa, whoa! Back up a bit there. Children of *Cain*? Now, I didn't take R.E., but even *I* know he was the first murderer in the bible? You're saying that he cre-ated you? A murderer?"

He shakes his head. "No. Cain was the first of us. He was penitent after slaying his brother, Abel. Our cre-ator made him the first vampire. The blood of his brother created the first werewolf."

And, once more, here we are again in Crazy Town. "Werewolf?"

The Creep nods. "But, they are all destroyed now. Rather publicly, I have to say."

I'm frowning. "Look, if there were a load of werewolves suddenly killed, I think I would know. Wouldn't that sort of make the news?"

"It did. At the end of January."

Weird, weird, weird. "No, it didn't. Can't you see how ridiculous that sounds?"

"And that is why humanity did not realise what was happening even though it was right in front of their faces. Excuses and reasons were made; people moved on."

I'm shaking my head for what feels like the millionth time.

"Whatever. So, what now?"

The Creep sighs. "Humanity needs a stronger signal that things are moving faster now. It needs something that it can't dismiss."

I *really* don't like the sound of where this is going.

"You promised you weren't going to hurt me…"

His woolly hat bobs up and down as he nods. "Absolutely. It's not you that needs to be the symbol, the beacon.

"It's me."

Chapter Four

Okay, so let's recap.

One: I've been abducted by a vampire.

Two: That vampire says he is actually here to protect me.

Three: My boyfriend was a monster sent from the future to wipe out humanity.

Four: My parents are the same as my boyfriend.

Five: I have a twin brother called Alec.

Six: Alec and I are special but my abductor/protector doesn't know why.

Seven: My life now sucks!

"So, what happens now?"

The Creep inclines his head. "It's busy out there now. There's quite a crowd gathering."

I frown. "What do you mean?"

"It would seem that the news of your abduction has caused quite a storm." He nods. "There's even a reporter out there with a camera. The police are doing what they can to keep people back but there are just too many onlookers, curious to see what's going on."

"People? Reporter? Police?"

He nods.

"But… how?"

The Creep pulls a mobile phone out of a deep pocket in his grubby overcoat. He slips off a padded glove, revealing an elegant hand, and taps at the screen. "Here," he says, handing the device over to me.

I take the mobile and I look at the screen. It's open on a social media post. In it, he's stated that he's got me and given our location. It includes a tag for the local television station.

"You… you *want* to be found?"

The Creep nods.

"Why?"

"As I said, things are gathering speed right now. People need to know what's coming. Justice was right. We've been hiding in the shadows for far too long…"

"Justice?"

"He was our king. He was killed last year by a construct."

"Oh." It's all I can say. I mean, what else would be suitable?

"He tried to make people aware of our existence," the Creep continues, his voice low and sounding sad again, "but it wasn't enough. Then, when the Bloodline was eradicated so publicly, we thought that would accomplish what Justice had failed to do. But you are a resilient breed. You shrug off the supernatural as just something rather *odd*. I suppose that's to be expected in this modern world of trick photography and special effects. It really does make me feel old."

"How old are you?"

"I was made a vampire in Victorian times. I'm approximately one hundred and fifty years old."

And, just when I think I'm getting my head around what's happening, he says something like that. How am I supposed to fully grasp that someone is genuinely that age?

"What do you look like?"

The Creep's dark glasses look around, making sure that he's not in a patch of sunlight, and he first removes his hat and then the bandages before slipping off the glasses.

He looks how he sounds: cultured. He has grey hair and a neat moustache. Intelligent grey eyes study me in the half-light of the abandoned warehouse.

"You don't look a hundred and fifty," I say.

The smile that I have sensed before is now apparent on his face. "Thank you, Amanda. I shall take that as a compliment. This is how I looked when I died as a human and became what I am today."

"A vampire?"

"A vampire, but so much more." He swaddles his head in the bandages once again. He lifts the woolly hat, strokes it with a gloved hand and leaves it lying on the dusty floor.

I can feel a tingling sensation at the back of my neck and I chew down on my lower lip before asking, "What do you mean by that?"

"*The Bloodline shall die, the Harbinger shall burn, the Light shall waken. When these three things occur then you shall know that they who are one will battle and angels will walk the Earth.* The first of the signs has occurred. The Bloodline perished. The second now needs to come to pass. The Harbinger must burn."

There is a sudden sinking sensation in my stomach. I really don't like where this conversation is going.

"What exactly do you mean?"

"When we are born to our new life we all suffer a terrible dream. It is a vision of how we will die. At least I know that my death will not have been in vain." The Creep… *Marcus*… rises to his feet and walks towards the large door at the end of the room. Glimpses of his shadow stretch out behind him as the sun squeezes its way in between treacherous cracks.

"What… what are you doing?"

"What has to be done."

"But it will kill you."

"I died a long time ago, my child. Death holds no fear for me."

No, no, no… This can't be happening. This makes no sense at all. I can't let him die like this. "Wait!" I call out. "You said I was special. You said that you were here to protect me. How can you protect me if you're dead?"

The bandaged face turns towards me and grey eyes dance in the dusty gloom. "Others will come. They will find you and care for you. Right now, I have to do what I must."

I sit paralysed as he opens the large door and walks out into a cacophony of noise. Questions are being hurled at him, demands are being screamed through what sounds like a loudhailer. Quietly, calmly, he ignores it all. Slowly and methodically, he begins to unwrap the foul-smelling bandages as he cries out:

"I am the Harbinger!

"I hear the Eternal Song!

"Find the Eternals! Protect the Twins! Await the Divergence!"

And then, without warning, there is an inferno in the doorway. I can't look. I simply can't. I bury my face in my hands and cry.

And, that's how the police find me.

I'm aware that there are people next to me. I hear them saying my name and asking me if I'm alright. There's a weird, distorted voice. It must be a walkie-talkie or something. Then I feel a gentle hand on my arm and I'm being manoeuvred up from the floor. As I rise unsteadily to my feet, I spot something lying on the floor and I bend down to scoop it up.

It's Marcus' old woolly hat. It's dirty and battered. It's all that's left of him.

I hold it tight as I'm escorted out of the old, abandoned building. I turn my eyes away from the pile of ash that lies in front of the gawping crowd of onlookers, all snapping pictures and videos with their phones. All the while, a gentle female voice is saying things to me, but I just don't listen. What she's saying is meaningless now. Someone just burst into flames in front of me. Nothing she says can put my life right now.

I am aware of another voice. A male one this time. I'm handed over to another officer and he guides me past the crowds and the eyes towards an awaiting police car. He opens the door for me and I climb mutely inside before it slams shut. The officer settles himself in the driver's seat and the car begins to move.

It's only after we have left the crowds behind us that I look up and see the back of his head.

And his neck.

There is a tattoo there of a black dragon.

I have to get out of here!

I sense movement and see his green eyes staring back at me in the rearview mirror before he pulls to a halt at a set of traffic lights. I take my chance and yank on the door handle. The handle does nothing. It just waggles back and forth in my hand. The door refuses to open.

The creature in front of me snorts in contempt and he turns the car down into a quiet road.

Then stops.

I look around me frantically, sure that he has stopped in order to kill me, but I see something most curious. There, in front of the car, is a cloaked figure, simply standing in the road.

The fake policeman swears loudly and shifts the car into reverse. He slams his foot down on the accelerator in an attempt to get away, but the car refuses to move. The engine is roaring in protest but we aren't going anywhere.

The reason for this is that the cloaked stranger is holding onto the front of the car.

Then, there's a loud grating noise and the door next to the driver is suddenly missing. An arm reaches in and drags him out. I hear a scream, then an awful silence. There's a rattling at the door next to me and it swings open. I'm greeted by the smiling face of a pretty blonde woman in her twenties. She winks a blue eye at me from beneath a huge hood before she is elbowed out of the way by another woman, also wearing a cloak. This one has short red hair and green eyes.

"Well, Scorp," she says. "It looks like the kid is safe and sound."

"But probably terrified," comes a male voice. A third cloaked stranger steps into view and the two women immediately step out of his way. His face is warm and kind. He has sandy brown hair and chestnut brown eyes. "Hello, Amanda," he says. "Everything's going to be alright now."

His name is Dave. Dave Nichols.

I am sitting with him in the back of a fancy-looking black SUV as Tigress (that's the redhead) tears through the streets of Sale, shouting abuse at other drivers, most of them who are clearly doing nothing more than sticking to the speed limit. The other vampire is called Scorpion. She just sits quietly in the front passenger seat.

"A bit of an odd name for a vampire, isn't it? Dave."

The male vampire looks somewhat embarrassed. I'm guessing that, if he had a pulse, he would be blushing.

"Sore topic," Tigress calls over her shoulder as she bumps up onto the pavement to skirt around waiting traffic. Horns are blaring in protest but she just ignores the complaints of the other motorists. "We're supposed to choose our own names once we're born to this life. A sort of tradition, as you were. But buggerlugs there can't seem to decide on one. Ow!" Scorpion has just pounded her on the shoulder. "Okay! Okay! I keep forgetting. He needs respect now he's our king."

I think my chin almost hits my lap. "You're a king? You don't look like one."

Dave shrugs. "My mother, Nightingale didn't look like a queen. It's what you do with a title that's important, not the title itself."

My eyes drop to my lap where I'm still holding onto Marcus' old hat. "Marcus told me about your mother. I'm sorry for your loss."

I feel his hand on my shoulder and look up into a warm smile. "Thank you, Amanda. That's very kind of you. It's been a hard few weeks, to be sure. Night's death is the least of our worries."

There's a harsh cough from the driver's seat.

"Nothing you need to concern yourself with, though," Dave continues to smile. But the smile doesn't really reach his brown eyes.

"Where are we going?" I ask, changing the subject to hopefully something less awkward.

"A safe place," Dave explains. "Our base of operations, so to speak."

I have all manner of places going through my head as Tigress nips through the streets of Sale. Is it an abandoned warehouse, similar to the one where Marcus took me but tricked out with all sorts of gadgets and tech to use in the secret war against the constructs? Perhaps it's a huge manor house on the edge of town with guard dogs patrolling the perimeter to keep out intruders? Or... Or... perhaps...

The car screeches to a halt and we get out.

"Are we here?"

Dave nods and heads over to The Bank, the pub that stands on the corner of Curzon Street and School Road. The one where the old winos spend most of their days.

"But... it's a town centre pub. I was just down the street yesterday, getting my hair done. I buy my lattes from the Caffè Nero over there."

"What can we say, Kid?" Tigress grins. "All these years we've been looking for the Twins and one of them has been living right under our noses for the past sixteen years. It's a small world when you think about it."

I look to Dave.

"She has a point," he smiles as he opens the door for me.

I walk through into the gloom of the bar and wrinkle my nose. It smells awful! It's like the time, a couple of years back, when I was invited to a party for this girl in my English set. I didn't really know her. Hell, I can't even remember her name now. But, I decided to be charitable and go along, even if only for an hour. Well, it was at this dreary little place over in Altrincham. Apparently, it was owned by her uncle, although God alone knows why she would have admitted to it. I lasted five minutes before I claimed to have a migraine and had to excuse myself.

I can't fall back on that one right now.

I point at an old guy with a red nose. He's sitting at the bar and has a mangy-looking terrier curled up at his feet. "Why's he got a dog in here?"

"It's not just *any* dog," Tigress whispers in my ear.

"No?"

"Uh uh. It's a special construct-hunting dog. It's got a heightened sense of smell. Can sniff them out ten metres away. Go on. Give it a go."

"What do you mean?"

"Let him sniff you."

"But, I'm not a construct."

"So, you'll be fine, then." She inclines her red hair in the direction of the squat little mongrel.

I chew on my bottom lip and approach the guy with the dog. Carefully, I crouch down and offer my hand to the dog's nose. It immediately lunges forward and starts barking and biting at me.

I lurch back and fall onto my rear, my stomach feeling like I'm going to throw up. "Oh my God! Oh my God! I'm one of them, aren't I? Don't kill me! Don't kill me!"

I hear a resigned sigh from beside me and feel Scorpion's arm settle around my shoulders as she pulls me carefully to my feet. I flinch back but she just shakes her head and then glares over at Tigress who is slumped on a bar stool, rolling with laughter. The silent vampire takes my hand in hers and squeezes it before leading me quickly to a small door at the back of the bar.

Tigress barges past and pushes open the door, still laughing her head off. "Your face! Your damned face!" she hoots.

"Is she always like this?" I ask the quiet blonde.

Scorpion nods and shrugs in mute acknowledgement.

"She's an acquired taste," Dave apologises from behind as he ushers me through the small door. "You'll get used to her in about two hundred years or so."

The room that I'm standing in now is immediately more pleasant than the one we've just exited. For starters, it smells better. There's no stale beer or dog sweat! It's smaller with a bar down the far end. A white-haired woman is standing behind the counter pouring out a pair of shots. Tigress goes up to her, says something and returns with the drinks, handing one to Scorpion. They both down the shots in one before wandering back over to the bar.

One thing which feels very odd is that all the eyes in the bar are turned in my direction. There are about seven or eight other people in here, who I'm guessing are all vampires, and I am their sole attention.

Dave steps up behind me and coughs loudly.

All eyes are suddenly looking elsewhere.

"It's what you do with the title, right?" I whisper.

"I'm so sorry," he replies, leading me over to a round table at the edge of the bar. "I can't begin to comprehend what it is that you're going through right now."

I just sit, shaking my head.

A plate appears on the table in front of me. It's been

placed there by the white-haired woman from behind the bar. "Welcome to Vixen's Den," she smiles. "I'm Vixen and I'm guessing that you're someone whose world has been turned upside down." She points to the plate. There is a bacon sandwich on it. "However, your body still needs nourishment and I could hear your stomach rumbling from all the way over there."

I open my mouth to protest that I'm not hungry but my stomach audibly disagrees. Instead, I say, "Thank you," and start to eat the sandwich.

I'm halfway through and something strikes me. I lay the food back on the plate and ask Dave, "How come there's food here? Don't you guys *not eat*? Isn't it just a diet of…" I grimace. "*You know what*?"

His easy smile appears once again on his face. "You mean, do we just go around drinking neck juice?" The vampire shakes his head. "No. We don't. Well, we're not *supposed* to. We were designed to hunt down constructs."

I nodded. "Marcus told me that."

A cloud falls across his face. "What else did he tell you?"

"It… It was all very confusing. I don't think he was of a sound mind. I think something really bad happened to him."

Dave nods. "I know. Scorpion saw it."

I gasp. "She was there?"

"No. Not like that. She has a gift. She sees things others can't. That's how we knew where to find you. She had a vision."

My eyes wander over to the blonde vampire. She's dancing slowly to the jukebox. Her arms are around the neck of Tigress and they are very close to each other, moving as one. "Are they a couple?"

"Indeed they are. They have been for over two thousand years. Tigress is actually the oldest vampire on the planet."

My attention turns back to the understated man in front of me. "So, why isn't she your queen?"

"It's hereditary. My lineage goes back to Cain in a straighter line than hers does."

I nod.

"But," he smiles again, leaning forward, "in answer to your previous question, we don't have to eat, but we do anyway because we enjoy it." In a movement faster than my eyes can capture, his fingers shoot out and steal a piece of bacon from my sandwich. Slipping me a wink, he gobbles up the morsel and licks his fingers clean.

I burst into uncontrollable tears.

I'm aware of a commotion in the bar. There are hushed questions as to whether I'm okay or not and an arm slips around my shoulders, pulling me into a soft embrace. Between my tears, I see long blonde hair and guess it's Scorpion. Her fingers gently stroke my hair."

"Damn it, Dave! Sorry, *Your Majesty*… what the hell did you do?"

The male vampire just stutters helplessly.

"It… It's okay." I sit up straight and try to smile at the irate Tigress. "It's just… my Dad." I swallow. "The *thing* that pretended to be my Dad used to do that every morning." I can feel the tears welling up again. "How? How couldn't I know? They weren't human!"

Tigress' features soften and she slips down onto the seat next to her partner. "You couldn't, sweetie. No one can. No *human* can anyway. Constructs are made to look and act just like every other mortal on this planet.

Only *we* can spot them."

"How?"

"Well, there are different methods, but the main giveaway is their smell. To us, they smell worse than soiled Victorian undergarments that haven't been washed since Disraeli was Prime Minister."

I pull a face.

"I know," she grins. "Gross, right?"

I frown. "Mike, my boyfriend was one. He always wore this strong aftershave."

Numerous heads around me nod. "It's a common diversionary tactic," Dave explains. "What's the matter?" he asks as my hand flies to my mouth.

"My… *parents*… What if they find out where I am?"

The vampire king exchanges a knowing look with his subjects.

I swallow. "They're not going to be able to find me are they?"

He shakes his head. "They'll never be able to look for you. You're perfectly safe here with us."

Chapter Five

The sun is streaming through the curtains. I can feel it stroking my cheek as I begin to wake up. I stretch, yawn and open my eyes. It's good to be in my own bed. The fluffy duvet feels just right to my touch. I scrunch it up around me and snuggle down for a bit longer, truly relishing the experience.

The window is open and a bird is singing outside. I can't see it from where I'm lying but its little tune is so pretty.

"Cheep, cheep, cheep... Cheep, cheep, cheep..."

Over and over, it sings its little heart out.

Just for me. So sweet.

I lie here for quite a while, just listening to the little guy enjoying the spring morning, until I decide that I really ought to get up. Pulling the wonderful duvet back, I swing my bare legs over the side of the bed. My feet slide effortlessly into my warm slippers that lie waiting for me on my plush cream carpet.

Floof, the giant teddy bear that Mike won for me last summer, sits happily on my armchair. I stroke the top of his furry head and recall Mike's shout of joy when he managed to knock three coconuts down in a row. I bury my face in the bear's soft fur so that I can inhale the remnant of my boyfriend's distinctive aftershave.

I draw back and cough. Urgh! Perhaps Floof needs a bath? He's smelling a touch rank right now. Never mind, Mum will sort it for me.

"*Cheep, cheep, cheep… Cheep, cheep, cheep…*"

I wander over to the bedroom window and draw back my patterned curtains. Looking through the double glazing at the long garden outside, I try to spot the singing bird, but it's nowhere to be seen.

"*Cheep, cheep, cheep… Cheep, cheep, cheep…*"

I close my eyes and let its song wash over me. It's so beautiful, almost hypnotic. I feel myself start to sway from side to side as it envelops me.

"*Cheep, cheep, cheep… Cheep, cheep, cheep…*"

Yes. It's calling out to me. It knows I'm near and it can sense me. It wants me to hold it in my hands to feel its soft feathers as its little heart flutters against its chest. It wants to wash over me with its beautiful, all-encompassing song.

My nose twitches and the spell is broken for now.

My stomach rumbles as the aroma of bacon reaches me. I grin, turn, pull on my fluffy dressing gown and pad downstairs. Mum is in the kitchen, busying herself at the stovetop and a glass of juice is waiting for me on the counter. "Hey, Sweetie!" she calls over her shoulder as she flips the bacon. "You sleep okay?"

"Mmhmm," I reply as I swallow the juice. "Absolutely." I'm such a sound sleeper. I never have dreams or nightmares. There are no monsters in the cupboard or my Physics teacher dressed up as a clown. Why should there be? My life is perfect.

Just like the song of that little bird.

"*Cheep, cheep, cheep... Cheep, cheep, cheep...*"

The kitchen window is open, allowing the warmth of the spring day to flood in along with the song of the little chap.

"*Cheep, cheep, cheep... Cheep, cheep, cheep...*"

I smile and Mum brings over my bacon and eggs. "Isn't it beautiful?" I say.

She chuckles. "It's just breakfast, Princess."

I shake my head and laugh. "No. I mean the bird."

"What bird?" She turns to the sink in order to start washing up. As she does so, she stands by the open window.

"*Cheep, cheep, cheep... Cheep, cheep, cheep...*"

"That one. There. Can you hear it?"

Mum inclines her head as she pulls on her pink rubber gloves. "Can't say that I can."

"Morning, Princess!" The familiar scent of Dad's strong aftershave wafts over me as he kisses the top of my head whilst pinching a slice of bacon off my plate.

"Morning, Dad," I chuckle. It's a good job that Mum always makes an extra slice. He does this every day. It's part of our little routine. "I was just talking to Mum about that little bird."

"*Cheep, cheep, cheep... Cheep, cheep, cheep...*"

Dad pushes his purloined bacon into his mouth before asking. "What bird, Princess?"

"*Cheep, cheep, cheep... Cheep, cheep, cheep...*"

"That one. The one singing in the garden."

He cocks his head and listens.

"*Cheep, cheep, cheep... Cheep, cheep, cheep...*"

"Can't say that I can hear it. Perhaps you can hear the radio. Did you leave it on upstairs?"

I lay my cutlery next to my plate and frown. "No. No, it's not the radio. It's a bird. It's out in the garden singing the sweetest song. I don't know what type of bird it is, I've never heard it before, but it sounds so beautiful."

My dad turns to my mum and asks her if she can hear the bird.

"*Cheep, cheep, cheep… Cheep, cheep, cheep…*"

She just shrugs and carries on with her washing up. Dad starts getting his stuff ready for work.

Ah, well. It's not a crisis. I turn back to my plate and see that there is no bacon. Dad had taken the only slice.

"Don't worry, have one of mine."

The dark-haired boy sitting on the opposite side of the counter takes a strip from his plate and offers it to me.

"Thank you," I say and place it on my plate.

I hear a small laugh and look up from my new breakfast. "What?"

"Seriously? That's all you're going to say? *Thank you*?"

"I'm being polite. You gave me some bacon, so I thanked you for it."

"Sooo… no question as to who I am or how I got here then?"

"Should there be?"

He lets out a sharp puff of breath. "This is going to be harder than I thought."

"*Cheep, cheep, cheep… Cheep, cheep, cheep…*"

"There's that little bird again!" I cry out. "Mum! Dad! Did you hear it?"

They just busy themselves with their morning jobs.

"They can't hear it," the boy says. "They're not *made* to hear it."

I pop the last piece of bacon in my mouth, chew,

swallow and ask him, "What do you mean?"

"Amanda, they're not like us."

"Duh! They're adults!"

The boy mutters something under his breath as he shakes his head. Then he looks straight at me with his blue eyes. "That's not what I mean." He grimaces and runs his fingers through his mop of unruly hair. "I should be able to sense you but there's something in the way. Something blocking me."

"*Cheep, cheep, cheep… Cheep, cheep, cheep…*"

His eyes look over towards the window and he nods. "Idiot. I'm an idiot. That's it, of course."

"That's what?"

He turns back towards me, his face excited. "You're near the Blade. You have to be. That's what's blocking me. Which means…"

"What? What does all this babble mean?"

His face darkens. "You're with *them*."

I turn and strangers walk into our kitchen: three of them. Two of them are women, a blonde and a redhead. The other is a man, tall with sandy brown hair. My parents stop what they're doing and an edge of concern creeps into their faces.

But, that's not all.

Their faces start to change. It's as if they're beginning to melt.

"Mum? Dad?"

"Amanda." The boy reaches over the counter and grabs my hand. "You need to wake up. Right now. Please."

"What? What do you mean?"

The three strangers are walking purposefully towards my parents. My parents whose arms are becoming longer than they should be. And, their fingers… Their fingers are melting together.

"Trust me," the boy urges. "You don't want to see this."

"What? What's happening?"

"Amanda. Please! Wake up!" he screams across the counter as the three strangers leap through the air and land upon my metamorphosing parents. The attackers drag their prey to the floor and ram their faces into their necks. My parents scream in agony and terror.

I leap from my stool but the boy's grip tightens on my wrist. "Let me go!" I'm screaming. "I have to save them."

"Amanda, you can't!" he shouts at me above the horrid sounds of my dying parents. "This… This is just a dream. I'm in it because I'm trying to find you."

"*Cheep, cheep, cheep… Cheep, cheep, cheep…*"

There's the birdsong again, still beautiful even as my parents lie on the floor having their life sucked out of them. How can it still be so beautiful? I want to go to it, to hold it in my arms.

It's calling to me…

It's so strong.

It blocks everything out with its song.

I cry out in pain and look down at my hand. The boy has impaled it with a kitchen knife.

"The hell?"

"Amanda, focus! Focus on my voice! I *will* find you, but it will take some time. I am nearby, but it's tricky. The Blade is so powerful. Just, one thing before you wake up."

I frown. "What?"

"You can't trust them."

"Who?"

He nods towards the three strangers who are now kneeling in a pile of dust that used to be my loving, caring parents. "Them. You cannot trust the Children of Cain."

I'm awake.

Truly awake.

My heart is in my throat and I'm gasping for air.

I rub my hand.

This isn't my bedroom. This isn't even my house. I haven't just watched my construct parents be devoured by the three vampires that rescued me.

The boy. He was familiar. I close my eyes and see his features again: a dark mop of hair and bright blue eyes.

"Alec," I whisper. My twin brother. He's coming for me.

I sit up. I'm on an old sofa. The vampires brought me up to this room late last night so that I could sleep. There's an ancient television on the opposite side of the room. A pile of DVD cases sit next to it on the floor. At first, I was worried that one of them was going to offer me their coffin but it turns out that's just a myth, something concocted by an over-active imagination of a Victorian author. No. No coffins. Apparently, they don't even sleep. Not normally, anyway.

"Our king, there, seems to like the occasional nap," Tigress explained as she dug some blankets out of a closet. "Not sure why. But if the sofa smells of geek, that's why."

I didn't get the reference then and I still don't understand it now.

There's so much that I don't understand.

I automatically go to pick up my mobile to check

what the time is but realise that I don't have it. I must have lost it somewhere along the way. To tell the truth, I don't actually remember having it since sometime before I stormed out of the hall at school after seeing Georgia kissing… *that thing.* The thought of the creature that pretended to be Mike turns my stomach.

Oh, God! I kissed it!

My stomach lurches even harder and I'm up on my feet, out the door and down to the small bathroom next door. I make it just in time before my supper from last night makes a return visit.

What the hell is happening to my life? It's not supposed to be like this! I'm supposed to be at school today. At least, I think I am. There's daylight coming through the bathroom window, so does that mean it's Monday? I think it does. Not that I've got a clue as to what the time is.

I spit grossness into the pan of the toilet and give it a good flushing before sitting down on the floor with my head lolling against the wall.

There's a gentle tap at the door. "Amanda?" It's a female voice.

I run my hand across my mouth and pull myself up to the sink. "Just a minute!" I call as I clean myself up. I look in the mirror behind the washbasin and a sight almighty looks back at me. "So much for waterproof makeup," I grumble then turn to open the bathroom door.

The concerned face of the white-haired Vixen greets me. "Hey," she smiles uncertainly. "You okay?"

I shrug. "Not really. You got a glass of water?"

The vampire smiles, nods and leads me downstairs. "Don't worry," she reassures me. "I've taken the precaution of shutting up for the day. It's just the *old faithfuls* here at the moment."

By, "*Old faithfuls*," she means Dave, Tigress and Scorpion. The three of them are sitting at a table in the barroom and seem to be having a heated discussion. "What's up?" I ask as I join them. "Problem?"

"Isn't there always?" Tigress complains, leaning back in her chair and stretching her legs out in front of her.

Vixen places a glass of water next to me on the table. I thank her and she smiles before heading off to the bar. The clock up on the wall behind it says five thirty! I've been out such a long time. I turn back to the three vampires at the table. "What's wrong?"

"Tigress is just complaining that every female Chosen One in literature and media is always blonde," Dave explains.

"Damn right it is!" the redhead explodes. "Every… single… time!"

Dave shakes his head. "That's just not true."

"Bull! You watched *Buffy The Vampire Slayer* recently? Don't… just don't answer that. Of course you have. Then there's that, 'Save the cheerleader. Save the world,' nonsense."

"You mean *Heroes*?"

Tigress nods. "Damn right, I do. They didn't have a redhead or African American in that cute little get-up, did they?"

"No…"

But Tigress isn't done. "The Bionic Woman. Blonde."

"Jamies Sommers was hardly a Chosen One. Plus, the remake starred Michelle Ryan, who was dark-haired."

A rude noise escapes from Tigress' lips. "Like anyone pays attention to remakes…"

"Well, sometimes they can be better. Take *Battle-*

star Galactica..."

"There's another one!"

"I thought no one paid attention to remakes..."

"I know, but there's that sexy thing in the red dress!"

Scorpion raises an eyebrow.

"Sorry, Scorp, but you've got to admit, she's hot."

The blonde vampire smiles and nods.

Dave is shaking his head. "Caprica Six wasn't a Chosen One."

"My arse, she wasn't! She started the whole she-bang off and some version of her was there at the end, still looking hot, I have to add."

The male vampire frowns. "Wait. Does this mean, you've actually watched *all* of *BSG*?"

Tigress shifts uncomfortably in her seat. She draws her legs under the chair and leans forward. "Well, your DVDs were just lying there and you kept banging on about how the Cylons were like constructs... Plus... You know... I love me a hot blonde." She blows a kiss at Scorpion who returns the gesture. "Okay. here's another, then. This one is *definitely a* Chosen One. That girl who looks permanently startled in *Once Upon A Time*. Emma Duck or whatever her name is."

"It's Swan," Dave sighs. "Emma Swan."

Tigress slaps the table with the palm of her hand. "There you go. Blonde again."

"Yes, but..."

"Oh, oh!" Tigress seems to really be on a roll now. "Then there's that program you watch when we're not around. The one with all the dragons and boobs."

"You mean *Game of Thrones*? I don't just watch it when you're not around!" Dave protests.

Tigress and Scorpion share a knowing look and

both dissolve into fits of giggles: Scorpion silently, Tigress raucously. When she's brought herself back under control, the redhead says, "You know that's not true, *Your Majesty*. Watching that serialised sex romp whilst we're in the room would be akin to watching porn with your mother! But, that's beside the point. There's another hot blonde in that one, too."

"You mean Daenerys Targaryen?"

Tigress nods.

Dave grimaces. "I take it you've not watched it to the end, then?"

The female vampire shrugs. "What's there to see? Blonde hottie in a dress with dragons: Chosen One!" She leans back in her chair and holds her hands up in what is a distinctly *go-bite-me* attitude.

I take a sip from my water and the glass makes a dull *thunk* as I set it back down on the table. The three vampires seem to remember that I've joined them.

"Oh, hey, Amanda," Dave smiles warmly. "You okay?"

The image of the three beings in front of me devouring my construct parents is starting to creep back into my head. I swill it away with a large sip of water. "Just tired," I say. "So, what's all this about?"

The sandy-haired vampire chuckles. "Oh, it's silly, really. We were discussing you. Nothing bad!" he reassures me as he spots the concern on my face. "We were just going over what we should do now. Anyway, as I said, Tigress here made the daft comment that all female Chosen One characters are, like you, blonde."

"Oh, I wouldn't know."

He shifts around and leans towards me, his face animated. "Well, it's quite simple really. There are loads of non-blondes. Take Wonder Woman for example. Did you know that she was actually based on…"

A loud groan from Tigress draws Dave's explanation to a sudden halt. "Seriously? You think this youngster cares about your comics?"

Dave looks flustered. "But…" He cocks his head in question to me.

"Sorry," I apologise.

That smile appears on Dave's face again. "It's okay. I get carried away, sometimes."

"So, you said that you were discussing me. Did you come up with anything?"

A silence falls across the table. It's Tigress who breaks it. "Kid, it's a weird one. We've spent thousands of years looking for you and now… Well, here you are. It's a big change. We're not sure what we should do with you. It's not like we can send you back home to a loving family and drop by with cake every now and then."

I swallow and begin to chew on my lower lip.

I drink more water.

Dave says something that I don't hear over the sound of screaming constructs.

"Sorry, could you repeat that, please?"

"I asked if there was something that *you* would like to do while you're with us. You must have so many questions."

I stare down into the glass that is now nearly empty. There's just a trace of water in the bottom. It looks like the glass of water that I used to keep on my bedside. I lift my hand from the tumbler and study my fingers.

"Actually, there *is* something."

It's a couple of hours later now. The sun has just

gone down and I'm standing out in the yard behind Vixen's Den with Scorpion. After I made my request, both Tigress and Dave said that they ought to be the ones to help me. This led to an argument. A loud one that seemed to go on forever. Things really are quite tense between the two of them. I get the feeling that Tigress just sees her new king as a child and incapable of ruling the other vampires. As a result, she's constantly kicking back at him.

Finally, while the two of them sat there and squabbled, Scorpion simply stood up, slipped her hand in mine and led me outside.

"They always argue like that?" I ask as I stand at one end of the yard whilst the quiet vampire moves things out of the way, giving us a clear space.

She smiles and nods.

"Doesn't it drive you nuts?"

She gives a little head incline and raises an eyebrow a fraction as she walks back towards me with a confident and assured gait. When she reaches me, she takes my hands in hers and studies them before offering me a frown.

"I... I don't know how it works or why. I just think I should be able to control it."

She nods in agreement and stands to one side, gesturing that I should see what I can do. I nod and start to flex my fingers. "Okay. Here goes." I thrust my hands out in front of me. Nothing happens. I try again. Still nothing.

I frown and look over at Scorpion. She twists her index finger in a circular motion.

I nod and push my hands forward. This time, I screw up my face and really concentrate. I'm imagining that my hands are actually on fire. I read once that if you really envision something, then it will actually come true. Some people even write stuff down on a board to make things happen. I think about burning the door in my dream. I recall my hands on fire when I was with Marcus. I remember the river bubbling at my touch.

I feel like I'm going to have a freaking stroke!

Nothing.

There's nothing.

I scream in frustration.

I hear a sharp intake of breath and look at Scorpion. She is staring in awe at my left hand. There, at the tip of my index finger is dancing a little flame.

I squeal in joy and it vanishes.

My brown eyes catch the excitement in Scorpion's blue ones. I turn back to the empty yard and fling my hands forward again.

Nothing.

I cry out in frustration and feel a sudden heat on my fingertip.

I lift the flame in front of my face and smile. It vanishes.

I feel empty. So empty. Why isn't this working? I walk over to Scorpion. "It's no good," I say. "I can't do it properly."

Scorpion wraps her fingers around my forearms and squeezes.

"I… I… can't. It's like there's a trigger, but I don't know what it is."

She moves her right hand from my arm and cups my cheek with her cold fingers. Her blue eyes stare intently at me and she frowns. She removes her hand and taps with a finger at my chest.

"What do you mean?"

The vampire steps back and pats at her own chest with her hand before shrugging in a questioning gesture.

"You want to know how I feel? Fed up."

Scorpion shakes her head, her blonde hair bouncing off her shoulders. She rolls an index finger backwards before pointing at my hands.

"Oh. You mean, how did I feel when my hands caught fire before?"

She nods.

I think back to the old warehouse. "Marcus and I were alone," I say, recalling the events. "He had taken me away. I was scared. Very scared. He was rambling. He was acting as if Nightingale was there." I see a melancholy look pass across Scorpion's face at the mention of the other vampire. "I had to escape. I had to get away. But he was in the way and I… I hated him. Yes, at that moment, I hated him more than I've ever hated anything before in my entire life."

A smile spreads across Scorpion's face and I look down at my hands. Tiny flames are now dancing across every fingertip. I smile and they vanish again. She gestures for me to do it again. I nod and think about Marcus, about him ranting and raving in the old warehouse. I think about him abducting me.

Then I think about him giving his life as a symbol of what he believed in.

I rub a stray tear from my cheek.

"I can't. Not about Marcus. He was good. He was just… broken."

Scorpion nods. She waggles her hands in front of her.

"Anything else?"

She nods.

"I don't think…"

But, there is, isn't there?

"I'm not sure…"

I can still hear the screams. The screams as my life is ripped apart.

"Scorp, I'm not sure this is a good idea…"

My life ruined by the being that I'm with right now.

"Scorp… I don't feel so good…"

My life torn to shreds by those my twin brother said I shouldn't trust.

"I… I…" Everything feels so distant as the anger builds up inside of me.

Something happens. Something snaps.

Everything is aflame and then there's darkness.

Chapter Six

I ache. Oh God, I ache. My eyes open and I'm lying back on the sofa again in the room above Vixen's Den.

What happened? How did I get here?

I was… outside.

My… hands.

Fire!

"Scorp!" I sit bolt upright. "Scorpion!"

"And, someone's awake."

That voice. I know that voice. I turn my head toward a chair that's in the corner of the room. There, sitting leaning forward with his hands clasped together is a man with dark hair. He is wearing a black denim jacket and dark glasses. There is what would best be described as a wry smile on his face.

"It's you," I say.

"Indeed it is," he smiles.

"You were in my dreams."

"I get that a lot."

My words have dried up. I'm not sure what to say now. I don't *feel* like I'm in danger, but there's something about this man. There's something very unsettling.

I chew nervously at my bottom lip before asking, "Where are the… *others*?"

"The vampires?" He chuckles slightly at my obvious relief that he knows about the Children of Cain. "It's okay. I'm up to speed with them. We go way back. Oh, and Scorpion's fine. Just a few burns."

I look him over again. I don't think I've ever met someone who radiates so much confidence. It's like someone has taken our school rugby team when they're heading out onto the field to play against the team at the bottom of the league and multiplied it by infinity.

"Who are you?" I finally ask.

"What does your heart tell you?"

"I'm not sure. Right now, it's kind of running around the room screaming."

His smile broadens into a toothy grin. "Great metaphor. Love it." He sits silently for a moment, simply watching me from behind his dark glasses. With a nod of his head, he finally says, "Why don't I show you something? That okay?"

I nod, albeit rather hesitantly.

The man holds out his hand then revolves it around and produces a dancing flame in his palm.

"Know someone else who can do this?"

My head stutters a nod and there are tears starting to form in my eyes.

"Hello, Amanda. I'm your father."

"My father?"

He nods, the fire still dancing in his palm.

"How can I be sure? Something else claimed to be my father before."

The man moves his fingers and the flame miraculously changes shape. It becomes one of the monsters from my nightmare. The one where they chased me up the tower. "The construct," he says. "The vampires told me. I'm so sorry that I wasn't there for you. Or your brother. You were stolen from me when you were babies. When you were newborns, in fact."

My fingers are fussing at the edge of the blanket that must have been lain over me when I passed out. "There's something you're not telling me," I say, my mind running around trying to work out what it is. Then it hits me. "You haven't properly introduced yourself. You haven't told me your name."

And there fades away the smile.

"Perceptive. Just like your mother." He snuffs out the flame and runs a hand over his clean-shaven chin. "Okay. So, it's important that you keep an open mind here. Please, don't freak out. It won't achieve anything."

I fuss harder at the blanket.

He takes a breath. "I'm Lucifer."

I stop fussing. "Okay. What's your surname?"

"Pardon?"

"Your surname. What is it? Mine is technically Harper as that was the surname of my so-called parents. But, I'm guessing it's really whatever yours is."

He frowns. "I... I... don't have one. I'm Lucifer."

"Yeah, I get that. That's your Christian name, but *everyone* has a surname. Even rock stars. They normally just go by their Christian name but they'll still have a surname. So, what's yours? Ours?"

He leans back in his chair, his face a mixture of confusion and amusement. "Seriously? You don't know who I am?"

I shrug. "No. Sorry. Are you big on YouTube? If you are, I can't have come across your channel. To be honest, the whole goth thing… Not really the sort of thing I look up."

There's a very weird silence in the room as he just stares at me oddly. Then, without warning, he brays with laughter and removes his glasses as he rubs at his eyes. I have no idea what's so funny. Eventually, he calms himself down and looks straight at me as he holds his glasses in his hands.

His pupils are on fire.

"I am Lucifer. I am the Light that came before all Creation. I am a Seraph, an angel that dwelt in the Heart of God and my song of worship forged the Realms. I was betrayed and fled from Heaven."

"Okay," I say. "If you say so."

His fiery pupils twinkle with curiosity. "Seriously? You're not winding me up here? You've never heard of me."

"I didn't take R.E.," I explain. "I took Art and P.E."

His face erupts into that grin again. "Then you have some serious catching up to do."

I nod. "I totally agree."

"How about somewhere more," Lucifer twists his lips together as he looks around the room in a decidedly unimpressed fashion, "stylish?" He clicks his fingers and there is a loud cracking noise.

Oh, wow!

We're no longer sitting in the room above Vixen's Den. We're in a cafe and…

"Is that the Eiffel Tower out there?"

Lucifer nods. "I thought we'd go somewhere where your face won't be popping up on the local news." He signals to a waiter who bustles over and takes his order. An order he gives in fluent French, I might add. Far more impressive than when Laura and I used to order baguettes from that little boulangerie near her parents' holiday home.

"I ordered you a latte," Lucifer says. "I get the impression that's your drink."

I nod. "Thank you."

"Trust me when I say that it's my pleasure. This… this must be very strange for you, I guess. However, you have no idea how weird it is for me as well."

"In what way?"

"Oh, dear Lord," he murmurs. "Where to begin?"

The waiter's back with the coffee. I've never had service this quick in Caffè Nero! Oh God, it tastes amazing. Lucifer's got this little espresso in the tiniest of cups which he sips from before taking a deep breath.

"Okay, so, for starters, in *my* life, we've already met. And I don't just mean when you were a cute and adorable baby. I mean," he waves a hand at me, "as you are now."

"But, I don't remember."

"You won't. It hasn't happened for you, yet. It's in your future but in my past."

I sip some more of my amazing coffee. "Are you, like, a time traveller?"

He waggles his hand back and forth. "Not exactly. Let's just say that I've been around the block a couple of times."

"Okay. So where, or rather *when*, did we meet?"

His face darkens and he leans forward, putting his elbows on the table. "After the Divergence, in the Divergent Lands." He nods as he sees the recognition on my face. "The Children of Cain told you about it?"

"Marcus. He said that a guy named Kanor will unleash his army of constructs."

Lucifer nods. "It's not pretty."

A silence hangs between us.

"Do we win?"

"I don't know. I've been asleep for a good long time. My memory is fuzzy at best. I know that, *this* time around, I've been on Earth for thousands of years. Right since the dawn of Humanity. I tried to train them so that they'd be able to fight, but they…" He shrugs and sits back in his chair. "I guess they outgrew me.

"Before that… Well, I was in the Divergent Lands, but all my memories of it seem to be lurking behind a huge fog. All I can really remember is that you were there, as was Alec, your brother, and Eloise, your mother."

"I've met Alec," I say.

For the first time, I see stunned surprise on Lucifer's face. "Really? When?"

"He came to me in a dream. He said that he's looking for me."

Lucifer strokes his chin. "Interesting. Yes, that would be about right…"

"What do you mean?"

"Well, in *his* timeline. We've just parted company, shall we say."

My latte pauses on the way up to my mouth. "That sounded ominous. What happened?"

"There was a *misunderstanding*. Did he tell you anything about your mother?"

I shake my head. "It wasn't, you know, a social visit. I had a dream about her, though. Alec and I were little and living with her somewhere very hot."

"I understand. That was a sort of memory of what *should* have happened. Constructs abducted you right after you and your brother were born. Neither of you got to live the correct childhood, but it still calls out to you. It did so to Alec, too." He sits quietly for a moment. "Eloise is, quite simply, amazing. She shares the same power as your brother: psyche. She can look into people's minds and can even manipulate what they see. Sometimes she goes around as this prim and proper librarian. Totally hot, let me tell you…"

I nearly choke on my latte.

Lucifer chuckles. "Too much info from your Old Man?"

"You could say that."

He smiles warmly and his dark glasses seem to study me. "You look just like her, although you have *my* eyes." He chuckles as my hands jump in front of my face. "Don't worry. There's no fire in there. I meant my colourings." He leans forward again. "There is one small difference between you and Elle, though." He twiddles his fingers and a small flame appears on his fingertip. He flicks it across to me and it lands on my hair. I gasp as I feel it running over the blonde dye. "That's more like it," he says, sitting back and admiring his handiwork.

I look over to a wide mirror that hangs behind the bar where baristas go about their job of brewing amazing coffee, unaware that an angel is sitting in their midst. I gasp as I see streaks of red amongst my blonde.

"Why did you do that?" I snap.

"Because it's who you really are."

"How the hell would you know! You've not been here. I hate these streaks. Hate them! They got me teased when I was younger." I slouch back and try to sink down into my chair.

Lucifer frowns. "Amanda, we are what we are. We

should never, *ever* let anyone try to dictate to us that we should be something else. That we should conform."

"That's easy for you to say. You're a freaking angel."

"And you're my daughter. What do you think that makes you?"

Well, that pulls me up sharp. It hadn't crossed my mind. "You mean I'm…" I look sheepishly around the cafe before mouthing the word and flapping my hands surreptitiously.

"Not exactly," Lucifer grins. "Your mother was created as an angel, but she was human when you were conceived." He holds up a hand as I open my mouth to ask a question. "Long story for another day. But the long and short of it is that you and Alec are both half-angel.

"What's more, you have the gifts that go with it."

I grimace. "I can't control mine yet. Alec seems to be far more powerful than me."

"Don't beat yourself up. It will come, given time. I was able to teach Alec how to start to master his skills."

"Okay. You'll do the same for me?"

Lucifer finishes his coffee and notes that my latte cup is empty. "I think it's time we were heading back."

There's a loud cracking noise and we are standing in the bar of Vixen's Den. The vampires are there and they rise to their feet as we appear.

"Scorpion!" I cry out as I spot the blonde. I run over and throw my arms around her. She hugs me tight then pulls back before her concerned eyes look me over.

"I'm fine, Scorp. Honest. You okay?"

She nods. I run a thumb over a singed patch of skin on her cheek.

"Sorry about that."

She waves a dismissive hand.

Tigress wanders over and slides an arm around her partner. "Scorp's made of strong stuff, Kid. Trust me, she's been through worse. Don't you worry about her. It's good to see you up and about. You had us worried. You were out cold for a whole day!"

"It certainly seems that you've made yourself some friends here," Lucifer smiles.

"They've looked after me."

"I should hope so, too. It *is* what I told Cain to do, after all."

Wow! Big reveal! "Wait? You're the one that turned Cain into the first vampire?"

He waggles his hand. "Sort of. Let's just say it was a younger version of me." He reaches into the breast pocket of his jacket and pulls out a battered packet of cigarettes. Slipping one between his lips, he lights it with the tip of his finger. "Amazing," he groans. "Truly amazing."

The vampires slip each other a quick glance.

"I know. Bad habit. Just started but been doing it for millennia."

There's not really a lot you can say to that, is there?

Lucifer blows two streams of smoke out of his nostrils, stands up straight and unkinks his back. "Right, then. I believe my daughter isn't the only precious thing you've located for me."

I'm back upstairs again. This time, I'm with Lucifer (I can't bring myself to call him Dad — just seems a bit weird) and Dave. Dave is opening the closet from where Tigress got the blanket for me.

"Seriously?" Lucifer remarks between puffs on his second cigarette. "You've kept it in a linen closet?"

"Not like I had anywhere else to safely stow it," Dave protests.

Lucifer gives one of his small chuckles and makes a beckoning motion with his hand.

The vampire reaches in right to the back of the closet and grunts as he apparently locates what he's looking for. Slowly, he pulls his hand out. In his grip is something long and wrapped in cloth. He brings it over and lays it carefully on the sofa that has been my bed for the last couple of nights. Without a word, he unwraps the cloth and exposes the most amazing thing I have ever seen.

It's a huge sword!

"*Cheep, cheep, cheep...*"

I look over at the window.

"*Cheep, cheep, cheep...*"

There's nothing there.

"*Cheep, cheep, cheep...*"

I'm sure I can hear the bird. It's the same one from my dream.

"*Cheep, cheep, cheep...*"

"Amanda?"

"Can you hear it? The bird?"

Lucifer finishes his cigarette. He crushes it between his thumb and finger before burning the butt to ash. "A bird?"

"Yeah, a bird. I heard it the other night too. In a dream."

He strokes his chin. "Interesting."

"What? What is it?"

"I want you to listen to the song, for me."

"Okay."

"Cheep, cheep, cheep…"

"I can hear it, but I can't see the bird." I walk over to the window. "There's nothing there."

"Are you sure that's where the song's coming from?"

"Cheep, cheep, cheep…"

I listen again. Carefully. He's right. It's not coming from the window. It's coming… from the sword.

Lucifer nods. "Okay. That's good. Now really concentrate. Listen to what it's actually singing."

I stare at the sword, at its shiny metal surface that glimmers in the low light of this small room. I listen again.

"Cheep, cheep, cheep…"

No. Not that. I don't want to hear that.

"Cheep, cheep, cheep…"

No! Stop it! You're not a bird. You're something else.

"… … …"

I gasp and Lucifer nods for me to continue.

I listen harder and, this time, I feel the song inside of me instead of hearing it in the room. It's warm, seductive. It wraps itself around me and draws me towards it. I feel my feet take a few awkward steps forward of their own volition. Dave makes to stop me but Lucifer holds a hand to the vampire's chest.

"… … …"

There it is again. That song, that rhythm. I can hear it, but I just can't make out the words. I desperately need to know them, to *understand* them. My hand is reaching out. It wants to stroke the surface of the sword just as I would a puppy.

"We…"

I feel like I'm transported somewhere else.

"Are..."

My bare feet are walking through infinite white halls.

"One!"

And I gaze upon this thing of beauty as it hangs suspended with its counterpart.

And I hear it tell me their names.

"The Cup and the Blade," I whisper. And I'm back here in a room above a pub in Sale. I feel an arm around me as I stumble. "What... what is it?"

"It is one of the Eternals," Dave explains. "It has existed since before even Heaven was created. Before Time itself. They were there before all of Creation."

I turn to Lucifer. "Just like you."

He nods and kneels down on the floor before the Blade. "Hello, old friend," he whispers before closing his eyes and cocking his head to one side. After a short while, he opens his eyes and nods his head. Getting to his feet, he wraps the Blade back up in its cloth. To Dave, he says, "Right, I have a job for you. I believe you're already familiar with All Saints Church in Wellington?"

The vampire nods.

"You're to take the Blade there and give it to the curate."

Dave looks stunned. "I beg your pardon? You want me to do what?"

"You have perfect hearing." There is a touch of menace in Lucifer's voice. "You don't need me to repeat myself."

"I heard. I just don't understand."

"The Blade needs to be there. The curate, one Peter Lincoln, will be its guardian."

"But... but, a human?"

Lucifer's lips twist up in amusement. "Now, did I say he was human? He's actually the Archangel Michael."

Dave's jaw has just dropped open.

Lucifer ignores the vampire's shocked response. "I think you'll find him most *interesting*. Take Scorpion and Tigress with you. Amanda can go with you as well. Make sure you keep her safe. Keep her with you at all costs."

Okay. What's going on here?

"Can't I stay with you?"

"Amanda, I have to leave and, where I'm going, I'm afraid you can't follow."

"No! No! You can't leave me. I've only just found you."

He steps forward and cups my cheek in his hand. I feel small flames flicker softly across my skin and I lean into his touch. "And you'll find me again. It will be a long, long time from now, but you *will* find me."

I look up and see that tears of blood are trickling down his cheeks.

"I need you," I hear myself saying. "Someone has to teach me what to do. I don't know what I am anymore."

"That's simple. You are a remarkable young girl with an incredible future. You will bring something amazing into this world."

"What? What is it?"

"I'm sorry, but you'll have to follow that adventure as it unfolds. Trust me, time travel's a bitch." He steps back and wipes the tears from his face.

"Amanda…" It's Dave's voice and his hand closes gently on my arm.

"DON'T TOUCH ME!" I scream and all the frustration, anger and despair of the past few days wells up in me. Dave backs off as the room is suddenly illuminated by a whirling ball of fire in my right hand.

I stare down at the small inferno then up at Lucifer who flips me a quick salute before saying, "There's Daddy's little girl."

Then he snaps his fingers and vanishes out of my life.

So, now I find myself in the back of the stupid SUV once more and, again, my life sucks...

"I'll wait here while you go and drop off your stupid sword."

Dave does that thing where it looks like he's sighing but he isn't really because he's dead and doesn't need to breathe. His arm is on the roof above the back door to the car and he's leaning in. The moonlight shines down on him and his skin looks whiter than ever. "I can't let you do that, Amanda. Your father said that you had to stay with us."

I just glower up from the back seat. I'm not going to make this easy for him. It's the day after Lucifer paid us his little visit before dashing off to God knows where. I've had a continual shadow following me around Vixen's Den; they've all taken it in turns to watch over me. It's so stifling.

What's more, I think they've forgotten what it's like to be human.

It's little things, you know?

Food, for example. Sure, they feed me. But, on the whole, I have to remind them. And then it's normally whatever is kicking around the Den. I'm starting to look like a bacon butty! I swear to God I've put on two kilos...

Then there's the bed. No, let's rephrase that, the sofa. They don't possess somewhere proper to sleep, so

I've been crashing on the sofa whenever I can. Obviously, they're up and about mostly during the night, so I've ended up being nocturnal, too. I'm starting to forget what the sun looks like and I've only been with them three days!

And clothes. Look at me! I'm still in the freaking school uniform that I wore to the *Kidsweek* fiasco! I don't even have a jacket, for crying out loud! The only thing I have that's vaguely keeping me warm is Marcus' old woollen hat. I snatched it off my "bed" before we left earlier this evening and rammed it down tight over my stupid hair.

I hate my hair!

Why did he have to do that?

Why couldn't he have left me alone?

Why can't they all just leave me alone?

"Well?"

I cross my arms across my chest and ignore him.

The so-called king of the vampires is replaced by the redheaded lunatic driver who got us here in well under the legal time that it should have taken. "Hey, kid! Stop sulking and get a move on. We've got stuff to do, people to see."

I ignore her and stare straight ahead.

"Screw this," Tigress grumbles and reaches in to grab me. She backs off quickly when the car is suddenly illuminated by a fireball in my hand. I watch out the window of the car as she stomps off to the main door of an old church, rummaging in a bag that she brought with her.

I continue to stare straight ahead.

There is silence at the open car door.

I turn my head just a fraction and squint out of the corner of my eye. Scorp is perched on the step up into the car, watching me with an amused smile on her face.

"I don't want to be here," I say.

The vampire just continues to sit there.

"I'm sixteen. I don't need babysitting."

I hear a cry of triumph from the porch of the church but Scorpion ignores it and just looks pointedly around the insides of the car.

"What?"

She looks up into the clear night sky and then back into the car. Bending in, she runs a delicate finger over the goosebumps on my wrist. She raises a perfect blonde eyebrow.

"Well, if someone had found me a coat, I wouldn't be cold, would I?"

She volunteers an apologetic shrug as Tigress calls something from the church.

Scorp offers me her hand.

I sigh. How the hell can I refuse her? Her face lights up as I climb out of the car. "Don't think for a minute that I'll enjoy a midnight visit to a stupid old church," I grumble.

Scorpion affectionately tousles my woolly hat and leads me over to the porch of the church. Dave throws me a glance as Tigress quickly stuffs what look like metal rods into her bag. She turns the handle on the door and it swings inwards. "Well, that was easier than last time," she grins.

"Last time?"

"Long story," Dave says. "Right now, we need to deliver the Blade and get out of here." All eyes turn to the long cloth package that he's carrying. It seems to be quiet for now.

"Why didn't you take it round to this guy's house?" I ask. "Surely it would be easier than breaking into a church in the middle of the night."

"There's something that Scorp and I wanna see," Tigress explains. "Something important to both of us. And it just happens to be in the church."

I sigh. Whatever. We enter the church; two vamps in front of me, one behind. It's dark and I bump into a long wooden bench. "Ow!"

"Watch where you're going, kid," Tigress snaps.

"Well, I wish that I could. It's pitch black!"

Dave walks over to the wall next to the porch and something clicks. The lights come on overhead. "Better?" he asks.

I just march over to a wooden seat and throw myself down. He doesn't deserve any thanks. Instead of showing gratitude that I don't really feel, I look around the church. What can I say? It's a church. It's old. It's cold. It smells funny. It's full of long wooden seats and there's Jesus up there on a cross looking very, very dead.

Probably died of boredom.

My so-called Mum and Dad never went to church. I guess it was the whole soulless lumps of clay thing. So, I never went, either. I don't see the point of sitting in a room with lots of people singing songs you don't understand and listening to some guy in a black dress talking at you for four hours.

The whole thing just feels rather weird.

Rather like the sensation at the back of my neck. I run my hand below the rim of Marcus' hat and shudder. I turn around and look at the back of the church. There's just some sort of big stone bowl there.

I stare at it.

Why the hell do I feel like it's staring back at me?

I grunt and turn forward, ignoring the stupid thing.

"Can't we go yet?"

Dave rolls his head around in a circle. "No. We have to wait."

"But it's cold."

Tigress shoots me a look of daggers. "Did we *really* have to bring her?"

Dave sets the cloth parcel containing the Blade down on one of the long seats and runs his hand through his sandy hair. "He said that I had to keep her with me at all costs, remember?" he explained. "I'm not to let her out of my sight."

Tigress sits down noisily on one of the wooden benches. "Jesus! Chosen ones these days."

Scorp has been leaning silently against the inside section of the porch. She pulls away, slipping me a wink, and goes to join Tigress. Crouching down, she runs her fingers through her partner's red hair.

"It's okay, Scorp," Tigress sighs over-dramatically, "I just don't like *babysitting*." She glowers in my direction as she says the last word.

I glower back.

Scorp just smiles, as she normally does. She reaches up and kisses Tigress on the forehead.

"Thanks, Babe," Tigress responds, stroking Scorp's cheek.

I've really had enough of all of this now. "Yuk! Will you two get a room? And I am *not* a baby."

Suddenly, the atmosphere around the three vampires changes. They are alert and are all staring over at the far end of the church, towards a long sort of screen that goes across the front of where we're sitting.

"Company," Dave whispers before Tigress transforms into a blur and thrusts her hand through the screen.

I hear a clatter and a grunt as she snarls menacingly, "Don't you know it's rude to eavesdrop, preacher-boy?"

I'm watching with a reluctant growing interest as something flies through the screen and lands with a crash on the stone floor of the church.

"Oh, you are so rude, preacher," the redheaded vampire tuts, still holding tightly onto her captive, "and when we've travelled so far to see you, too."

It looks like Dave feels it's time for him to intervene and he carefully approaches the commotion. "Tigress, please release our host."

The female vamp hesitates for just a moment. There's a definite look of annoyance on her face. She really doesn't like taking orders. "As you wish, *Your Majesty*." She lets go of whoever is on the other side of the screen and swoops down in a low bow before running off in a blur and sitting herself down on one of the benches with her boots up on the one in front of her.

I see Dave give a small shake of his head before he talks quietly to the person on the other side of the screen. There's a click and a wooden gate in the screen swings open. A man walks through. He's tall with dark brown skin and neat afro hair. He's wearing a black shirt and trousers, so I'm guessing he's the curate that we've come to see.

I can't say that he looks like an archangel. I guess I was expecting wings and a halo.

What he does look like, as Dave introduces himself and the others, is seriously confused. His confusion increases tenfold when Dave brings him in my direction.

"And this... Well, this is Amanda."

The priest stares at me with his dark eyes and I feel like someone is rummaging around in my head. I thrust my hands under my legs. I don't think now would be a good time to go all *flamey.*

Dave gives one of those infuriating smiles as he watches the priest's confusion. "That's right," he says, "Amanda here is different to us three. Or are we different to her? It's one or the other. I'm sure her father could explain it better than me."

"Her father?"

The father who waltzed into my life then ran off and left me with a bunch of strangers…

I sit harder on my hands. They're starting to warm up.

I hear Tigress cough and Dave says, "Sorry, can't go into that right now. But he sends his regards."

Well, the priest is looking even more confused now. He turns back to me and stares even harder. He's got a look on his face as if he recognises me somehow, but can't quite place me.

I, however, have just got very hot hands.

I glower at him and turn away, trying to think about not accidentally setting fire to the bench upon which I'm sitting. I just want him to stop staring at me. He's making me feel extremely uncomfortable.

"What do you mean she's *different* to you?" he asks without taking his eyes off me.

"Oh, you know…"

The curate spins around. Dave has moved faster than I or the priest can see and is now leaning against the stone bowl at the back of the church.

"Oh, *I know*, what?"

Then Dave is back next to the priest. He presses his mouth close to Michael's ear and whispers, "She's not a vampire."

The priest really doesn't like this. Nope. Not one bit. He does something with his hand and Dave is thrown down the far end of the church.

I do what any sane person would in this situation. I scream and dive down under my bench.

"Well, it sounds like you're having fun…"

I'm not the only person hiding down here. Alec is sitting with his back against the bench in front of me, a cheery smile on his face.

"How…?"

He taps the side of his head. "I'm not actually here right now. I'm inside your head."

I frown. "Do I have a concussion?"

"No. I've put myself in there. Just like I did in your dream. Oh, and when you talk to me, the others can't see or hear it, so they're not going to think you're crazy."

I snort in contempt. "I think it's more likely that they're the crazy ones."

Alec's face goes dark. "Obsession can do that to people."

"What do you mean?"

He blows air through his lips. "Long story for when we have more time. First, I'm in Sale. Where the hell are you?"

"Some old church. They did say, but I didn't catch where. I wasn't really paying attention."

He's rolling his eyes and groaning. "You've got to be kidding me. Is there a huge carving of Jesus on a cross and a big stone font with a weird inscription on it? If there is, then I've just come from there!"

"I don't know about the inscription, but the other two things match."

He nods. "It would make sense I guess. Everything

seems to lead back to All Saints. Why are you there?"

I tell him and his face looks even darker. I can tell he's seriously annoyed. "Alec, what's going on?"

"Tell you what, it sounds like things have calmed down. Let's stretch our legs."

I climb out from under the wooden seat and stand up. Looking over towards the vampires and Michael, I frown. Something's wrong. Something's wrong with Scorp.

"Amanda? What is it?"

"It… It's Scorpion. She looks sick." I make to go to her, but feel a cold hand on my arm.

"No. Trust me. Stay away from them."

"But, she's my friend. She's been kind to me."

"You can't trust them. Any of them."

"You say that, but why?"

Alec peers over in the same direction. He looks like he's straining to see through a dense fog. Eventually, he nods. "She's had a prophecy. She'll be fine."

"You've seen her do this before?"

My brother shakes his head. "Sam told me about it." He runs his hand through his mop of dark hair. "Walk with me."

I follow him to the back of the church, where he leads me to the big stone bowl. "What is this thing?" I ask.

Keeping a distance between himself and the bowl, he closes his eyes and seems to concentrate. At the edge of my hearing, I feel like I can hear rushing water.

"Alec?"

His eyes open. "It's a font, for baptising Christians when they become part of the faith. However, it's more. A *lot* more."

I wait for him to continue. As I do, I absentmindedly

tap a nearby bench with my toe.

Eventually, he says, "The best way to describe it, for now, is the door to a prison. There is an entity, a *thing*, that encircles our part of the universe. It's a river, an *ocean*, but it is sentient and it can see everything that has or will happen. It's called the Abyss and it likes to interfere. Our father had this font erected to trap her and prevent her from meddling. The inscription is sort of the key."

I read the five words: "*Knaves are not our responsibility.* What does that mean?"

"Read the initials."

"*K... A... N... O... R.* Kanor. I've heard that name before. Marcus mentioned it."

Alec shudders. "That's a whole other thing." He grimaces.

"What's wrong?"

"The Blade. It's really messing with my ability. We don't have much time. What's going on now?"

I look down the far end of the church. "The vamps and the archangel are going through a wooden screen to another part of the building. They're all talking."

"They do that a lot," Alec grunts. "Right, now's your chance."

"My chance to do what?"

"To get away from them. They're distracted. Get out of here and run. If you can get away from the Blade and the Children of Cain, then I can find you and come get you. We can finally be together."

His face lights up.

As does mine.

I reach out and wrap my solid fingers in his ghostly ones.

"I'd like that. A lot."

My twin brother is fading away as I creep over to the door where we came in. No one notices me as I walk quietly outside into the night. I guess they have other things that are more important to them, after all.

I choose a random direction and begin to run.

I'm doing this! I'm actually doing this! I'm getting away from all the craziness that has overwhelmed my life for the last five days, hell for the last few months since the dreams started. I'm going to be reunited with my brother who actually cares for me and will explain everything to me.

I can feel the reassuring pounding of my feet on the asphalt and I'm breathing in the deep, clear night air. I feel liberated. I feel released.

I pause to catch my breath.

I feel an arm grab me.

I feel a sharp pricking sensation in my neck.

I feel nothing…

Chapter Seven

Everything is pink. Pink and fluffy. I can reach out and touch it, everything that is, and it bounces against my fingers.

Hee hee. It's funny.

There. I've done it again.

Squish!

It's all a great big marshmallow. I like marshmallows. They're sooooo tasty. You pop them in your mouth and feel them slowly dissolve on your tongue.

Just like everything is doing around me right now. It's all dissolving. Everything. Slowly. Softly.

I'm falling back into it and dissolving with it. There goes my skin. There go my muscles. There go my bones - right from the longest ones in my legs to the tiniest, littlest ones right in the middle of my ears.

I'm all one with everything now and everything is one with me.

It feels…

…perfect.

How could I possibly want it any other way?

Wait. There are voices.

No. I don't want voices. I just want the peace of the pinkness.

But the voices are getting louder. They go, "Merph merph blerph. Plerph blerph terph…" It makes no sense. They are grabbing the pinkness and tearing it apart.

No! Stop it! Don't ruin the pinkness. It's all I want; all I need right now. How could I want anything else?

There are people standing there shouting at each other. "Merph merph blerph! Plerph blerph terph!" They are waving their arms at each other. I watch the pretty rainbows that trail after their shaking fists and pointing fingers.

One of the fingers points at me. It's attached to a woman I recognise from somewhere. I can't recall where, though. She's not part of the pinkness and the pinkness is all.

Her fingertip winks at me.

I wink back.

Someone screams and the whole world seems to turn around as I pirouette like a pretty ballerina on my toes.

I'm a swan! I'm a swan! Look at me, a swan!

There's shouting and screaming — so much shouting and screaming.

I see what looks like a big white freezer lying on its back. There are heavy chains next to it.

It makes no sense. It shouldn't be here. It isn't pink and swans don't need a freezer.

There's more shouting and someone comes running towards me. They're holding something. It's in their hand and all their pretty little fingers are melting, dripping off the glass surface that shines in the dim light of the overhead bulb.

I feel my hands become very warm.

There's more screaming.

There's a jab at my neck and the pinkness is whole once more.

Where am I?

I wasn't here before. At least, I don't think I was.

I'm sure I was somewhere else. Somewhere… pink?

Well, that's the furthest possible from here, that's for sure.

This place is… barren. There's countryside as far as I can see. No sign of a town or even a village. There are not even any trees…

How can there be no trees?

There are just vast swathes of empty land. The grass looks dry and unkempt. Bracken lines the muddy path along which I'm walking. I stumble and fall. I roll on my shoulder and cry out, but the baby is safe.

Wait, what now?

She hasn't even woken up. As I lie on the muddy road, I gaze down at the sleeping face of the baby.

My baby.

The world around me is ruined, scorched to oblivion, but perfection lies in my arms, gently snoring.

I pull myself up and kneel in the wet mud. Still, she doesn't stir. She just continues to sleep and her breathing is slow and rhythmic. I bend low and it sounds like music. No, it sounds like rushing water flowing over pebbles in a brook.

I could stay here, kneeling in the mud, for an innumerable amount of eternities as long as I have my baby in my arms and her song in my ears.

But we can never have what we want, can we?

I hear a familiar, terrifying sound and, all around us, the mud begins to come to life. Tall pillars rise from the ground and take on a ghastly shape of creatures with long arms and an absence of necks. Their arms reach out and grab at my child.

I won't let them have her!

They can't take her! Not after everything that I've been through. I drag myself to my feet and I run. I hurtle along the rutted track, my child tight to my chest and tears streaming down my cheeks.

They can't take her! I won't let them! I stumble and fall. Again, I roll, protecting my baby and again she does not stir.

The constructs loom up above us, surrounding us and penning us in.

They can't take her! They mustn't take her! Everything depends upon her. I close my eyes and feel the burning pressure of anxiety, frustration and anger welling up in the space where my child was nurtured for nine months. I nurture this second embryo, feeding it, fuelling it with all my rawest emotions.

And then I give birth to it.

The fireball rips out from its epicentre, scorching the ground beneath and baking solid the constructs as they grasp out for my child.

But that is not enough. Not for these child-snatching monsters.

I stand up, tall and proud, my daughter in my arms and feel the fire begin to boil within me once more. I feel all the times that I have been hurt, humiliated and betrayed. I give these moments in time form and substance. Then, as I scream out into the barren Divergent Lands with my eyes screwed shut, the fire mushrooms up from me, consuming everything in the immediate radius.

I open my eyes and dust motes drift softly on the air around me.

But still, my child and I are not yet safe.

A vast shadow falls across us. Its black wings stretch out across the horizon and obliterate the rays of the life-giving sun. A scream rends the air apart and I see sharp white fangs gnashing and chomping in a wide, hungry mouth.

The dragon swoops down and tries to gobble my child whole but I turn and run. This time my footing is sure and I keep ahead of the snapping and snarling maw.

He cannot have my baby! I will not let him.

So, I run and run and run…

The dragon falls behind, a thundercloud in a grey sky and I reach the end of the road.

There is a cottage. It is small and mostly ruined. Its thatched roof is patched with sticks and branches and the windows are open with no glass to protect its inhabitants from the elements.

A scream echoes from within and I feel nauseous to the pit of my stomach. I check on my baby, but she continues to sleep soundly, her melodious snoring her entire world.

I approach the cottage and enter through a shattered, broken door. The sight that I see fills me with horror and revulsion.

Someone is lying on a filthy bed. They are still, motionless. Blood is pooling from between their legs. There is the sound of a bleating little cry as a woman with blue eyes and blonde hair with red streaks cradles a small baby, tears streaming down her cheeks. Next to her feet, a small dog sits with its head low and its ears drooping.

I take a step towards the terrible sight and realise that my arms are empty.

Where is my baby?

Where is my child?

Where is…

"Eve," whispers the woman as she soothes the baby in her arms. She turns to the dog and says something that I cannot hear. A swirling circle of light appears behind them and they step through, taking my baby with them.

A door opens on the other side of the cottage and Alec enters.

"Amanda? Can you hear me?"

It's cold. I want to curl up and die.

I'm nothing without my baby. She's gone and I'm completely empty.

"Amanda! You in there?"

I look up and Alec is standing over me in an open doorway.

I say nothing. It's just another dream. How will this one break me?

He runs his fingers through his mop of dark hair then thrusts his open hand towards me. "Come with me if you want to live!"

"Pardon?"

"I said… Wait? You don't get the reference?"

I shake my head.

"Seriously? *T2* when the T-800 goes and rescues Sarah Connor."

I shake my head again before realising something. "Wait? This isn't a dream?"

A grin spreads across Alec's face. "Nope. It's a rescue."

I take his hand. It feels warm and secure. The world sways and he steadies me.

"So, first," he says, "a little housekeeping." Reaching out with his spare hand, he cups my cheek and his eyes stare intently into mine. I see a window thrown open in my head and a rushing gale sweeps through the dusty room within.

I gasp and suddenly everything is crystal clear.

"You came for me!"

"I said I would. Now, let's get out of here."

I pause as I spot a pile of mud-coloured goo on the threshold of the door. "Is that?"

"I convinced it that it was tired of existing. But there's plenty more of them around. We need to get out of here."

I frown as he leads me down a dimly lit corridor. The walls seem to be wooden and the roof is a corrugated metal. "I saw… I think I saw a freezer. There were chains."

"Later. First, we need to get out of here."

I pull to a halt and Alec jerks backwards as his hand is still in mine.

"Amanda. We need to get out of here."

"You're not telling me something. I don't like it when people keep secrets."

"It's not a secret. It's just… It's just that it's awful."

"I've seen a lot of awful recently. A little more won't make much of a difference."

My twin brother swallows. "They were going to chain you up in the freezer and dump you in the sea."

"The Hell! Why didn't they just shoot me or something?"

"If I said *Hoots, Mon, ye cannae die…* you wouldn't get that reference either, would you?"

I shake my head. "You're weird, you know that?"

He shrugs.

I smile. "But, I like it."

My smile evaporates as someone walks around the corner of the corridor. It's the woman who was talking to my so-called mother, in Sale. The one who was with the dragon tattoo guy. I instinctively make to cry out, but Alec whips his hand across my mouth and shakes his head. The woman is glowering and muttering to herself as she walks right past us. Not once does she stop and stare at the random teenagers in the corridor. What does catch her attention, though, is the open door to my cell. She darts in, then cries out in anger. In fact, it's safe to say that she turns the air blue. Bursting out of the cell, she hurtles back down the corridor.

"How?" I whisper once Alec removes his hand from my mouth.

"You have our father's gifts; I have our mother's."

At the mention of our mother, a flash frame of her standing, crying whilst holding Eve snaps into my head. I shudder and bat it away. I'll figure out what all that was about later.

I realise that Alec is talking. "We need to get out of here," he urges, pulling me down the corridor, this time in the opposite direction, away from where the construct ran. "I need to get you to safety."

I stop.

I stand.

I turn.

I face down the corridor in the direction that the construct ran.

"No."

"Amanda?"

"I said, *no.* I'm not running. Not now; not any more. I'm done with being the victim, with having my life dictated and prescribed to me." I can feel the heat of anger brewing within me. It's rolling around inside the void which someday will hold my baby girl. I feed it and fuel it. Upon the roaring flames, I throw logs of mistrust, betrayal, hurt and wrath. As the inferno builds, I stretch my arms to my sides and luxuriate in the sensation of the primordial element running through my veins and arteries, out towards my hands. I am flexing my fingers and I can feel the flames building in my palms.

"Can you survive fire?" I ask my brother.

"Probably. But it'll hurt like a bitch."

"Then you'd better run," I hear myself say as I step forward.

There's the sound of running footsteps before he pauses and calls out, "Give 'em hell!"

After that, I am lost to the fire.

As I run my fingers down the walls of the corridor, I feel it twisting and turning through me. The fire is me and I am one with the fire. The walls erupt into an inferno behind me, I am bringing Hell to this world at my touch. All those that stand before me shall burn. They shall pay for what they have done to me. I am aware of footsteps approaching. I raise a hand and the flames shoot out. Two pillars of smoke stand in my way. I step through them. They are nothing before me. The flames rage inside and I release them. My hands stretch in front of me and an all-consuming fireball rockets down the corridor of screams. It burns within my eyes and all I see is red. There is no other shade now. This is who I am. This is what I was born to be. I am fire incarnate. Movement becomes ash as fireball after fireball is released from me, torching all that it touches. The building is now completely aflame; it is one with me. We are both fire. We are both ablaze. Nothing can escape us as we reach out with our burning embrace and draw in anything that dares to move. All that which caused me pain will be gone soon; it will be purified in the mighty inferno that reduces all to ash. I reach out again and more are gone. Flesh becomes clay becomes pottery. I smash it with my arms as I pass by and I grind it to dust under my feet. I dance through the building searching out all those who feel they can hide from the flame. In rooms, in cupboards, up on the roof. There is no escape from their fate. I drag their soulless corpses to Hell. I damn them all to dust. Then, as I finally leave that place, my vengeance temporarily sated, I turn and stare at my handiwork.

And I smile.

Epilogue

The sun shines through the window of the first-class train carriage as we travel north. Alec tells me that it is the second of April. It has been five days since the *Kidsweek* disco at school.

I'd had no idea. Every day had seemed to merge into one — just a series of events lurching left and right over which I'd had no control. There was only one time when I truly knew where or who I was — when I finally wrenched back control of my life. That was when I released the fire within me and burned down the constructs' hideout.

When we left, there had been not a shred of material remaining. Nothing had survived the blaze.

That gave me a warm glow inside.

I doze most of the way north. When the guy comes round to check the tickets, they check everyone else's, but not ours. Alec goes to the buffet carriage and comes back with a mountain of food. I graze a little bit before letting the tiredness envelop me. I drift off to sleep, my head on my brother's shoulder.

And I dream of Eve.

I sit rocking my little bundle back and forth in my arms.

All the time, she snores that sweet little sound of a babbling brook.

All the time, I smile.

I awake once more on the journey. We are crossing a wide river. I tell Alec about the river from my dream of when we were little, about how my powers made the water boil and steam.

"I had that dream too," he says, a sad smile on his face. "It never happened, you know? The constructs abducted us when we were just a few minutes old. What we saw was what was *supposed* to have been."

I nod and I think of Eve. Is she what is supposed to happen? Will I give birth to her and carry her in my arms? Or will I lie dead in a derelict cottage as my mother spirits her away to safety?

Two trains later and I find myself exploring a strange city. "It doesn't feel very big," I say as we walk over a crossing onto a pedestrian precinct.

"It's not," my twin admits. "But what it lacks in stature, it makes up for in character."

I'm quiet as we walk down the precinct then turn right. I see an old horseshoe set in a paving slab. A few minutes later, we emerge into a busy square. Traffic trawls past and a green statue of some old woman is in the middle of a garden on the other side of the road. Alec guides me past a Chinese restaurant and through a door that leads up a flight of stairs. He unlocks a plain-looking door and we enter.

There is a man sitting at a dining table.

He turns towards us and smiles.

Author's Notes

First and foremost, thank you for buying my book and reading it all the way to the end. I hope you enjoyed it. I know that I certainly enjoyed writing it. I've always loved reading and writing short-form stories. From the reading point of view, they are something with which I can settle down in an armchair and a warm drink and lose myself in their content for a few hours before emerging with a new set of images and thoughts in my head. From the writing perspective, they are something that I can dive into with all guns blazing and create in a few days of frenetic activity, giving them a sense of freshness, possessing that creative spark as the story quickly emerges and characters evolve.

At the time of writing this, it is late in 2023 and this is the second novella that I've written this autumn. The first was the final chapter in the *Bobby Normal* series, *Bobby Normal and the Black Dragon*. Not only this but I'm mid-grand edit of my magnum opus *Fallen Angel* and sketching out ideas for 2025's Sam Spallucci book, *Dare The Dragon*. In short, I'm sat at the centre of a creative hurricane with ideas and plotlines whipping past me at terrifying yet exhilarating speeds. I am thoroughly enjoying myself as I take these ideas and start to bring them all together. We started to see this in 2022's *Sam Spallucci: Fury of the Fallen* but they will be expanded upon more in 2024's outings, *Child of Light* and *Sam Spallucci: Lux Æterna*. Sam's life is rapidly heading towards the events of the Divergence and the subsequent rise of Kanor. The suspects are starting to be lined up and it's for you, the reader, to try and point the finger at who you think might just be the devastator of humanity. As we travel along this path, the two novellas, *Child of Light* and *Child of Fire*, are very much signposts for where we should be looking as they are concerned with one of those mysterious tenets of the Children of Cain: *Protect the Twins*. Each of the novellas will accompany a novel (*Sam Spallucci: Lux Æterna* and *Sam Spallucci: Dare The Dragon*) giving extra information about the devastating results of those two books.

But, I get ahead of myself. Back to the book that you're currently holding in your hand.

Child of Fire had its origins quite a few years ago after I'd read a *Point Horror* novella. I can't for the life of me remember the title or indeed the story itself. It was something I'd picked up either in a charity shop or on one of these freebie bookshelves that you find dotted around the place. What I do remember was it being about a girl whose life wasn't what it first appeared and that I fancied a crack at writing something similar. It was certainly pre-*Casebook* and I was heavily into vampires at the time, devouring all that Anne Rice had to throw at me, so I sat down and started the novel *Halfling*. The plot was going to be something along the lines of a teenage girl finding out that her father was actually a vampire. I wrote the beginning of the novel — twice in fact. The first attempt had her miserable with her life as she started to have dreams about a mysterious man calling to her. The second attempt turned things on their head and made her current life idyllic.

And, that was as far as I got.

These two aborted starts eventually combined to become the start of the novella that you've just read. However, it was about two decades after they were first written that I finally wrote it. Over the intervening years, Sam's world developed and the notions of the Twins and Lucifer. As I wrote about Sam and his adventures, I was desperate to come back to this story. I knew that it could figure prominently in the Spallucciverse lore. So it was that after I finished *Lux* and was working on the final *Bobby Normal* book that I started to properly sketch out the adventures of Amanda, tying them in to stories I had already written in *Fallen Angel* and referred to elsewhere along the way.

If you want more details on the crossovers (and there are a lot!), then I suggest that you go check out my Easter Egg video on YouTube. There are links over on my website.

The biggest challenges for me were writing the book in the first person, nearly-present tense and from the perspective of a teenage girl.

First-person was a no-brainer as I love that internal narrative style, plus *Child of Light* was written that way and I wanted the two stories to match stylistically. The use of nearly-present tense (i.e. happening now or just a few minutes or seconds ago) became a necessity to keep Amanda, and consequently the reader, in the dark of what was happening to her as events unfolded. For example, at the beginning of the story, she doesn't have any idea as to what constructs are, let alone the fact that her parents and boyfriend are creations of Kanor. It also meant that we could see her absolute horror as people died or were hurt. I love the scene where Jack gets impaled. Amanda reacts so naturally, just as you or I would. It would be disbelief followed by sheer terror.

As for writing like a teenage girl… Well, I've read numerous Young Adult books and, to be honest, a lot of them suck. You get the odd gem but, on the whole, I'm not a fan of the genre. This is mainly because I feel that the characters do not react realistically or that the adults writing them are too distant from their own childhood. They see it with the old rose-tinted glasses and have forgotten just what it was like to be a teenager. All too often, the kids just accept what is happening and are completely okay with it. People who know me will know that it is my biggest criticism of the otherwise superb *Stranger Things*. At the beginning of the story, when Bill is abducted, his mates see it as a big adventure rather than crying themselves to sleep in terror. All too often, YA books are just unrealistic. I hope that in *Child of Fire* we see how Amanda is at times afraid and helpless but growing more and more annoyed with her situation as she slowly comes to terms with it through the pages of the book.

Is she based on anyone? Sort of. As well as being an author, I'm a private tutor and I've taught a lot of teenagers over the years. Certain mannerisms and things they've said have certainly crept their way into the character of Miss Harper.

Anyway, I'll leave it there as I'm sure you have other things to get on and do. Again, thanks for reading this latest outing of mine. If you get a spare moment, a review or rating on Amazon and/or Goodreads would be appreciated. If you have any questions or theories, feel free to reach out to me on social media. Links are all over on my website: www.aschambers.co.uk.

Take care and have a great day.
ASC March 2025.

About The Author

A.S.Chambers resides in Lancaster, England. He lives a fairly simple life of walking in the countryside, gazing at mountains and wondering if clouds taste of candy-floss.

He is quite happy for, and in fact would encourage, you to follow him on Facebook, Instagram, Threads, TikTok, Patreon and YouTube.

There is also a nice, shiny website:
www.aschambers.co.uk

www.ingramcontent.com/pod-product-compliance
Lightning Source LLC
Chambersburg PA
CBHW051708180726
48283CB00004B/1259